Available in August 2009
from Mills & Boon® Intrigue

Colton's Secret Service
by Marie Ferrarella
&
Rancher's Redemption
by Beth Cornelison

Sheikh Protector
by Dana Marton
&
Scions: Revelation
by Patrice Michelle

The Heart of Brody McQuade
by Mallory Kane
&
Killer Affair
by Cindy Dees

Loaded
by Joanna Wayne

Dark Lies
by Vivi Anna

Bodyguard to the Bride
by Dani Sinclair

DARK LIES

BY
VIVI ANNA

MILLS & BOON

First published in Great Britain 2009
Harlequin Mills & Boon Limited,
Eton House, 18-24 Paradise Road, Richmond, Surrey TW9 1SR

© Tawny Stokes 2007

ISBN: 978 0 263 87316 0

46-0809

Harlequin Mills & Boon policy is to use papers that are natural, renewable
and recyclable products and made from wood grown in sustainable
forests. The logging and manufacturing processes conform to the legal
environmental regulations of the country of origin.

Printed and bound in Spain
by Litografia Rosés S.A., Barcelona

Vivi Anna likes to burn up the pages with her unique brand of fantasy fiction. Whether it's in the Amazon jungle, an apocalyptic future or the other-world city of Necropolis, Vivi always writes fast-paced action adventure with strong, independent women and dark, delicious heroes to kill for.

Once shot at while repossessing a car, Vivi decided that maybe her life needed a change. The first time she picked up a pen and put words to paper, she knew she had found her heart's desire. Within two paragraphs, she realised she could write about getting into all sorts of trouble without suffering any of the consequences.

When Vivi isn't writing, you can find her causing a ruckus at downtown bistros, flea markets or in her own back garden.

For Shayla, Forever

Chapter 1

The moment Jace Jericho stepped into Boneyard's staff room, he knew there was trouble.

The entire crime scene unit was assembled. Lyra, their young witch, sat on the sofa, her petite frame rigid with nerves. The chief, Caine, leaned against the corner as if unaffected, his new wife Eve next to him, not quite pulling off the same impassive look. Her hand rested on his forearm in a sure sign of support and affection.

Jace still had a difficult time accepting that his best vampire friend had married a human. But it was obvious that Eve made Caine deliriously happy, so he didn't protest. At least, not out loud.

Kellen, the firearms expert, Gwen, the lab tech and

Dr. Givon Silvanus, the medical examiner, sat at the long wood table. Even the baron himself, Laal Bask, was present. He stood in the center of the room, trying to command the attention of the others. As usual, everyone on the team ignored him.

When Jace entered, Caine acknowledged him with a nod. "Thanks for coming in on your night off."

Jace shrugged. "It didn't sound like I had a choice."

"You didn't."

Settling in beside Lyra on the sofa, Jace glanced around the room. Everyone looked nervous, especially Eve. She kept her eyes on Caine; Jace could see the tension in her face and in the way she twisted her hands in her lap. Something major was going on and it had to be human-related.

Jace prayed they hadn't found another human body in Necropolis.

Caine moved to the center of the room to stand beside Laal. The baron took that as his cue to start talking.

"First of all, I'd like to thank everyone for coming in. I know some did so on their days off." He tipped his head to acknowledge everyone.

Caine cleared his throat. "Let's just cut to the chase, Laal. We're wasting time." Caine glanced around the room meeting everyone's gaze. "There has been another murder."

Lyra shivered beside Jace. He glanced over at her and saw a look of knowing in her big brown eyes. Her hand was on the silver pentagram amulet at her neck and she was rubbing her thumb over it. For comfort or concentration, he couldn't be sure. Had she had a vision? Was she having one now? Sometimes she knew things before the rest of them did. As powerful as his wolf senses were, Jace's abilities were no match to Lyra's.

"This one is very similar to Lillian Crawford's murder." Caine met Jace's gaze and kept it. He knew the vampire was trying to read his emotions. Trying to figure out if he was thinking about the last case. It had been horrific for everyone involved.

Caine continued, "The body was found in an abandoned house in San Antonio."

There was a collective gasp across the room. Even the devil-may-care vampire, Kellen, had a look of alarm on his tattooed face. No small thing, considering he usually didn't give a rat's butt about much.

"Who called it in, Chief?" Jace asked.

"Captain Morales phoned Eve." Caine glanced at his wife and gave her a small smile. "As a courtesy, he's asked us to come in and investigate."

"You and Eve?"

Caine shook his head and looked right at Jace. "All investigators are going in. You, me, Eve and Lyra. The rest of the team will be on standby in case we need them to process information."

A sense of dread washed over Jace. "Do you really think that's necessary? I'm sure they don't need all of us there."

"It is necessary." Lifting his gaze, Caine glanced

around the room. "If this murder is like the others, we'll need everyone's help. So, be on alert."

"When are we leaving?" Lyra asked.

"Right away. The crime scene's getting cold. So grab your kits and your gear. We'll meet in the garage in a half hour."

Everyone got to their feet and began to file out of the room.

"Remember to be on your best behavior out there." The baron clapped his hands together and smiled. "Your behavior is a direct reflection of this lab."

Everyone ignored him and exited the room, Caine and Eve the last to leave.

Jace remained seated. He wasn't going anywhere. It had been over fifteen years since he'd been in any human city. He wasn't going to one now.

When Caine reached the door, he glanced at Jace. Pressing a kiss to the top of Eve's head, he said, "Grab my kit. I'll meet you in the garage."

Flicking her eyes to Jace and then back to Caine, she nodded and left.

Sighing, Jace leaned back against the sofa. He knew what was coming even before Caine opened his mouth. "I'm not going. You don't need everyone there."

Caine stood in front of Jace with his hands in his pockets. The vampire's casual stance was deceiving. Jace knew that under Caine's spit and polish beat the heart of a formidable predator. Not someone a person would want on their bad side. Jace knew this was going to lead to a disagreement. They butted heads on a weekly basis.

"It isn't up for discussion, Jace. The whole team goes."

Standing, Jace brushed past Caine to pace the room. He had a hard time staying still for more than ten minutes at a time. It was even harder with the moon calling to him. It was close to a full moon and Jace should've been out running through the woods instead of being at work. That the lab was underground and didn't have any windows was a small blessing. At least he didn't have to see his pale mistress begging for him to come play with her.

"Who's going to run the lab?"

"Monty can handle it. He's not a complete incompetent ass."

Jace arched his brow. Everyone knew that the day supervisor *was* an incompetent ass.

Caine shrugged. "Okay, he is, but he can handle it while we're gone. Jace, there isn't an argument you can give me that's going to change my position on the matter."

"I can't do it, Chief. Not after all I went through. I can't be around them."

"We've all suffered in the past."

Jace stopped pacing and glared at him.

Caine put up his hand in defense. "Yes, some more than others. But you have to get over it, Jace. It's history."

"Not to me." Jace opened his mouth to protest further, but Caine kept talking. The vampire had a remarkably effective habit of doing that.

"You need to get over yourself and do the job. It's as simple as that." Taking his hands out of his pockets, Caine moved to the door. "I'll see you in the garage in a half hour."

Anger surged through Jace as he continued to pace. He hated being ordered to do anything. Especially something like this. He couldn't ignore what had happened and he couldn't forget.

Over the past few months, he'd been able to warm up to Eve, despite her being human. They weren't best buddies and never would be, but he could sit down with her and have a conversation. Sometimes even philosophical ones that he quite enjoyed. Of course, he would never openly admit that to anyone.

When she arrived in Necropolis to work the Crawford murder a few months ago, Jace had thought she was as useless as the rest of the human population. To his surprise, she turned out to be a good investigator and a good person. If Caine loved her, there had to be something remarkable about her. He figured she was an anomaly.

One human was tolerable, but an entire city? There was no way Jace could handle it. The plethora of smells and sounds alone would drive him mad. Sometimes his lycanthropy was a curse.

Caine cleared his throat. Jace had completely forgotten that he was still there. "You're the best investigator I have, Jace. I need you with me on this." Without another word, he left.

Sighing, Jace ran a hand through his scraggly mop of brown hair. The chief had an uncanny ability to make him feel commended and disciplined at the same time; when he was telling Jace he was doing a good job, Jace also felt the suggestion that he could do better. When it came down to it, Caine made him want to be a better investigator and a better man.

The fact that his mentor was a vampire and not a werewolf wasn't lost on Jace. He just shrugged it off as another interesting reason he loved living in Necropolis. The species that resided in the city certainly had their differences, but as a community they had learned to work around them. There were rules and regulations set up to protect each species.

In the human world there were no rules.

Pausing for a moment, Jace sat on the edge of the long wooden table and took in some deep breaths. He'd need to center himself if he was going to work with humans. He was a moody son of a bitch as it was. Being around a bunch of humans for more than a few hours was going to put him in a permanently foul state. He'd need some inner peace if he was going to keep at bay his urges to shift when he felt cornered or confronted.

He'd had six years to work on it since he'd been employed by the lab. The first year had been touch and go with Caine and the others on the team. He hadn't been sure if he would ever be able to work well with others. He'd shifted forms so many times in moments of anger that for a while everyone called him Wolf Jericho.

It had been Caine who had helped him with self-control. The baron had wanted to fire him the first time he'd shifted and pinned one of the lab techs to the wall, but Caine had insisted on giving Jace another chance. And another. And another. He claimed that, being a lycan, Jace had a natural gift for crime-scene work.

Jace could still remember his first case. The evidence he had found at the scene and processed in the lab had put a two-time rapist behind bars. It had been a rush to know that the work he did was the reason the police were able to get the violent criminal off the streets and into a prison.

After a year, Jace, as well as the rest of the staff, realized the chief had been right. He was very good at his job. Crime detection became his life. He breathed, ate and slept the job. He couldn't think of anything else he wanted to do. He still got a rush with every new case.

Except there was no thrilling rush with this case, only fear and hostility.

He didn't want to admit it to Caine, but he was afraid to go into San Antonio. What if they found out about him? About his gift of shape-shifting? What if this time, they didn't let him live in Necropolis with the others, but put him back into the freak show where he grew up? Jace knew he'd never survive something like that again.

Lyra shuffled into the staff room, rustling Jace from his maudlin thoughts. She regarded him with her generous eyes; her head was titled to the side like it often was when she looked at him.

Once he had asked her why she looked at him that way. She told him it was because his aura was so explosive and colorful, it was interesting to watch it swirl around his head like a rainbow tornado.

"I've come to fetch you," she told him, a little smile at her pretty mouth.

He smirked. "I was wondering who he'd send."

"Caine knows that you can't say no to me." She grinned.

"Are you okay with going?"

"I don't mind humans." She shrugged. "I'm enlightened, and hold no prejudices."

"Hey, I'm not prejudiced," Jace argued.

"Yeah, right." She smirked. "Are you coming? Or am I going to have to tell everyone in the lab that you're too chicken to go into the city?"

"Jeez, I'm coming." Jace pushed off the table and followed Lyra out of the room.

As they walked down the drab hallway to the elevators, Lyra glanced up at the ceiling in front of her. She nodded.

Jace knew she was having a silent conversation with her dead grandmother. It had been peculiar at first to watch the little witch converse with thin air, but Jace had gotten used to it. Especially after the time he scoffed at Lyra's ability to talk to the dead and an icy wind had nearly ripped his jacket off his body. And that night he suffered from very vivid nightmares of being chased around by zombies.

He never doubted her again after that.

"Is your gran saying something about me?"

Lyra glanced over her shoulder at him and shook her head. But he saw her shoulders stiffen then relax. And he saw the flicker of fear cross her face.

He tensed. "What did she say?"

"Nothing. She's just making small talk," she said. Her scent subtly changed.

She was lying. But he wasn't positive he wanted to know why.

Chapter 2

There was a crowd hovering around the abandoned house when Jace and the rest of the team pulled up to the curb in their black SUVs. Jace had no qualms thinking it was because of the guest investigators and not the murder itself.

Before opening his door, Jace glanced over at Lyra sitting in the passenger seat. She was staring at him.

She smiled and said, "Don't worry, I'll protect you."

"Bite me," he growled.

Chuckling, she opened her door and slid out.

He took in a few deep breaths. Already, his chest felt tight and his neck ached from tension. The drive to San Antonio had nearly killed him with the moon winking at him seductively through the windshield. But he had fought the urge to pull over, shift and race across the open land. Although even now, he could feel the moon singing to him.

He was unsure if he could hold it together if he looked up and caught the moon's gaze. He'd have to get out of the truck, grab his kit and get inside with his head down.

Taking in another deep breath, Jace opened the door. The refreshing night air felt like heaven on his skin. The odor of moldy, wet wood and putrid waste floated over him. It made him shiver with the need to escape.

He jumped out of the vehicle and rushed around back to grab his kit with his gaze glued to the ground. Once he had his hand wrapped tight around the handle of his stainless steel suitcase, he followed Caine, Eve and Lyra up the sidewalk to the dilapidated house.

They passed several uniformed cops going up the cracked cement walkway. Jace could detect a variety of emotions wafting off them. Animosity and fear were the major ones. But there was also curiosity. It smelled sickly sweet like corn syrup. That was the human response he hated the most.

The emotions he smelled now reminded him of the stinking filthy crowds that had paid to see him when he was a child. This crowd shared the same morbid curiosity that the others had as they had watched the poor little boy covered in fur stalk around his cage.

Shaking off the memories, Jace kept his eyes on Lyra's back as they entered the house. She glanced over her shoulder and gave him a half smile. He nodded at her in response.

Every since they had met, Lyra could always sense his moods. If the forensic team was a family, Lyra would be his little sister. They never missed a chance to rib each other, but when it came down to it, he knew he could always count on her to be there for him.

More cops were standing around as they moved through the run-down house. Jace hoped they hadn't contaminated the scene and that they were just there for a show. He hated when the cops traipsed through evidence without realizing what they were doing. It was a tough enough job collecting the primary evidence without having to pick through all the irrelevant stuff left by clueless law-enforcement personnel.

The smell hit him like a sledgehammer in the face when he followed the rest of the team into what would've been the living room of the gutted house. Blood. Death. Despair. And something else that he found odd. Sulfur. It was faint, but it was there.

Spotlights had been set up around the room in a triangle. All the light pointed in one direction, up, toward the center of the room. Jace heard Lyra's gasp and knew she had looked at the primary crime scene at the same time he had.

The victim, a young woman, was suspended from the ceiling by a rope wrapped around her ankles. Her slender arms hung lifeless, the tips of her long, blond hair skimmed the wooden floor. Her throat had been slit. Magical symbols adorned her naked torso. No blood pooled on the floor beneath her. It had obviously been drained from her and taken away. Just like in their last case.

Jace stepped in closer to the scene and stood next to Lyra. They were waiting to get the go ahead from Caine to examine the scene. The chief was talking to another man, a human. It was Captain Morales from the San Antonio crime lab. He had been Eve's boss when she worked for the humans.

Behind him stood a couple of uniformed cops. The stoic expressions on their faces radiated a sense of rivalry and territoriality. Something Jace knew quite well.

Caine shook Morales's hand. "Good to see you, Hector."

"You, too, Caine." He turned to Eve. Smiling, he shook her hand. "You look good, Eve. I wish it were under different circumstances, seeing you again."

"I think we all do, Hector," she answered.

Hector turned toward the crime scene. "Does this look the same?"

Caine nodded. "Except for the elevation. Our guy siphoned the blood with rubber tubing for quicker results. Draining the blood this way would've taken a little longer. A couple of hours, I'd say."

"Well, he would've had it. This neighborhood is mostly abandoned. A few residents live in the apartment complex across the street. But none that would speak up even if they did hear anything."

"Any ID?" Caine asked.

"No. Nothing on her. We'll run her prints at the lab."

"How was she discovered?"

Hector sighed. "Some young girl came in here to smoke up, must've seen the body and run out screaming. A patrol car almost hit her, a block over, when she jumped out in front of it waving her arms and sobbing."

"Where's the girl now?" Eve asked.

"At the hospital. The patrolman said she went into shock."

"I'll go to the hospital to see if she's talking," Eve suggested.

Caine nodded. "Good idea."

"Do you have someone that can take me, Hector?"

Captain Morales nodded, and then glanced behind him to a female officer. "Officer Sanchez, take Eve with you to the hospital."

Jace could hear the officer mumbling under her breath. It was in Spanish, but he didn't need to know the language to understand the meaning. He glanced over at the others to see if they could hear her. Caine's steely eyed gaze convinced Jace that he had heard her loud and clear.

Before Eve could take two steps, Caine grabbed her arm and pulled her to him. He hugged her tight and pressed a kiss to the top of her head. Jace knew he did it as a show of possession. Showing everyone in the room that if anything happened to Eve someone would pay dearly.

It was a purely lycan thing to do. Jace had always wondered how much of him, if any, had rubbed off on Caine. Obviously, some had over the years.

Eve followed the reluctant cop out of the room. Before she passed through the doorway, she looked back and nodded to Jace and Lyra. "Good luck."

Lyra raised her hand to wave. Jace just nodded back, the sounds and smells swirling around him too intense to do much else. He wanted to get at the body. The urgency to do his job sent pulses like electricity through him.

"Do we have a TOD?" Caine asked.

Hector nodded. "The coroner pronounced time of death to be between 9:00 p.m. and midnight."

"Are you sure we're not stepping on your toes here?"

"Hey, this is way out of my league, Caine. The minute I saw her, I knew you had to come in on this. Don't worry about stepping on anything, as long as we get this one solved." Hector scratched his chin, a five-o'clock shadow was starting to sprout. "The sheriff has given me some leeway. I've managed to quadrant off a section of the lab for your team. You'll have a couple of techs to do the grunt work, but you'll also have plenty of privacy."

"Thanks, Hector. I appreciate that."

Hector nodded. "Also, one of the officers discovered a metal drum in the backyard. Looks like something was burned in there recently."

"Okay. We'll start with the body and work our way out back."

Caine turned and glanced at Jace. He could sense Jace's impatience. Caine nodded. That was all the acknowledgment Jace needed to start moving. Setting his kit on the floor, Jace took out gloves and plastic shoe covers.

Once he took a step forward, Lyra followed suit. She was outfitted in two seconds flat and went straight to the body.

"Can we bring the body down, please?" Lyra asked.

Already anticipating the request, one of the uniforms rolled a scaffold ladder toward the victim so he could lower her corpse to the ground.

Jace started his evidence collection around the body, in a circle. Burnt black candles made this direction easy to follow as they were placed two feet from each other in seemingly perfect symmetry.

Taking up the camera that had been around his neck, Jace snapped pictures of each candle as he walked around the scene. Sulfur came to his nose again. Maybe it was just the result of the matches used to light the candles. But for some reason, he didn't think so. Matches did have a certain sulfurous scent, but not like this. Not this strong.

He glanced at Caine. "Do you smell that?"

"The sulfur?"

Jace nodded.

"From matches, maybe?"

"I don't know." Jace stepped back to his kit. "I wish we had something to collect the scent, an absorbent agent."

"Your nose is good enough, Jace. I trust it."

Once they had the corpse down, they moved it away from the actual crime scene and onto white sheeting they had placed on the floor a few feet away. Lyra took her pictures then raised her hands over the body and *felt* for a magical signature.

While Lyra was doing that, Jace bagged the candles one by one. When he picked one up on the northeast side of the circle, he found something imprinted on the floor in wax. He fixed his flashlight on it. It was a partial shoe print.

Setting a measuring card beside it, he snapped off a couple of pictures. "I got a shoe print."

"Can you lift it?"

Jace shook his head. "I'll have to cut out the floor and take it with us."

Reaching into his kit, he took out a sharp pocket knife, opened it up with his thumb and cut a six-inch square around the wax imprint. He lifted the thin plywood and slid it into a paper evidence bag, labeling and sealing it.

"Good eyes, Jace," Caine said from his perch beside the head of their victim. He was busy inspecting the neck wound. "There's no evidence of bite marks. If this was a vampire's work, he wasn't thirsty." He poked at the neck with his finger. "These look like slash marks."

Jace's head came up. "What?"

"Take a look." Caine stood as Jace came around the body and crouched.

His stomach flipped over as he inspected the deep slash in the victim's neck. It indeed looked like a claw mark, not a knife wound.

He cursed. "This looks bad, Chief."

"I've got a signature," Lyra said as she took a step away from the body and put her hands on her hips. "It's the same."

"Are you sure?" Caine and Jace asked in unison.

She nodded, then rubbed at her nose with the back of her gloved hand. "I'm positive. I memorized that signature. The feel of it is the same."

"But that's impossible," Jace remarked. "We got the guy, remember? Mel Howard confessed to the murders and he's dead."

She glared at Jace. "And I'm telling you it's the same."

Caine raised his hand to stop the impending argument. "Okay. We'll file it as evidence and see what we get with the rest. There's an explanation and we'll find it."

Nodding, Jace went back to searching the floor grid, but he couldn't shake the sensation of dread rushing over him like adrenaline. If it was the same magical signature, then something was going on that none of them had faced before. Something outside even the Otherworlder realm. Which was not a comforting thought at all. If they were supposed to be the monsters, then what in hell had killed this girl?

Bending down to bag a dark fiber, the hair on the back of Jace's neck rose to attention. A charged sensation skimmed the surface of his skin. He'd experienced feelings like this before, but only within the confines of Necropolis. And usually when he was around his lycan pack.

He stood and waited for the sensation to pass, but it didn't. Instead, it seemed to intensify. Was there a storm in the area? The sky had been clear when they drove into the city.

Glancing around, Jace tried to determine where the

sensation was radiating from. He looked at Lyra. Was she doing a spell? Is that what he was sensing, her magic? But when he watched her, he noticed that she was busy pulling fibers and whatnot from the mouth and nose of the victim, not incanting a spell.

So if not magic, what?

Captain Morales stepped into Jace's periphery and cleared his throat. "When you're done and need to go back to the lab, I have your police escort here. She's on loan from another department." He glanced behind him. "This is Tala Channing."

A lithe young woman stepped around Hector and nodded toward the team. Her green eyes flashed like emeralds in the glaring spotlights.

Jace found he couldn't breathe.

Chapter 3

Not prepared for the situation, Tala Channing watched in rapt fascination as the members of the Otherworld Crime Unit gathered around the lycan as he dropped to his knees. Was he having a heart attack?

She had read up on lycan physiology, well, as much as she could find in the meager pickings of local libraries, and every text had claimed that lycans were physically superior and healthy. That they rarely suffered from sickness. They couldn't have heart attacks, could they?

Jace Jericho certainly didn't look like a man that would suffer from heart problems. He had a powerful body. Even in the shadows of the house, Tala could tell he possessed a fine form. His T-shirt clung to his wide frame. His arms bulged with muscles, as did his legs, even under the faded denim of his pants.

Not that Tala had been staring at him. Her gaze had fixed on his for only a brief moment. It was just that he was very hard not to notice.

The petite, dark-haired woman, the witch on the team, Tala assumed, put her hands on Jace's forehead and on the back of his neck and closed her eyes. Tala thought the touch looked very intimate, something a lover would do. Not that she cared. She didn't even know the lycan, let alone harbor any feelings toward him.

But deep down inside, a tiny flare of jealousy ignited.

"What's wrong, Jace?" The vampire chief investigator asked.

Jace shook his head. "I don't know. I feel strange."

"Is it a spell, Lyra?" Caine asked the witch.

Opening her eyes, she removed her hands. "No. I don't feel any conventional magic." Her gaze swept the room and locked onto Tala.

Tala had the urge to back away. The witch's stare was penetrating. But what was she looking at her for? Tala hadn't done anything. She was merely following orders.

Jace pushed to his feet and rubbed a hand over his face and into his hair. "I'm fine. Must be all the smells in here."

"Gather all the evidence you collected and put it in your kit. You can take a look at the barrel in the backyard. That's probably where the perp burned her clothes. Then you can head back with Lyra to the lab and start processing with the lab techs Hector loaned us," Caine suggested.

"I said I'm fine," Jace growled back.

The hair on Tala's arms rose with the lycan's words. His voice made her shiver and not in an entirely unpleasant manner. There was a certain power in him and he affected her. She supposed she should've expected it.

"There's nothing more here to collect. I'll go back with the body." Caine clapped Jace on the shoulder, then turned to go back to the victim. "I'll see you at the lab."

Avoiding everyone's gaze, Jace retrieved his bagged evidence and shoved it in his kit. He marched past the crowd, who were trying not to look at him, toward the back door.

Tala watched him leave. She could feel the anger wafting off him like steam from a scalding shower. It floated over her, making her skin prickle.

She knew her assignment was going to be tough. As a transfer from another department, she expected a certain amount of razzing. It didn't help matters that unflattering rumors about the reason for her transfer followed her like a bad smell. Being a woman also didn't help. However much integration police departments had gone through over the years, and despite the publicity surrounding equality, it was still a boys' club.

This babysitting assignment was just an example of the kind of thing she knew she would be subjected to. Tala was told to prepare for animosity and strange activities and mood swings. That the Otherworlders might be difficult to handle. Difficult seemed like such a tame word to describe Jace Jericho.

Feral.

That was the one word that popped into her head when she first saw him. His chiseled face had been stern in concentration and his dark brown hair looked wind-blown, unruly, as if he had just come back from a hard run. Wild and untamed, he had that look about him. As if nothing and no one could pacify him.

Tala thought she had mentally prepared for this assignment. The minute after she was handed the order, she rushed out and did as much research as she could on each of the members of the OCU. The vampire and the witch she'd known wouldn't be problematic.

It was the lycan that had worried her.

Tala snapped back to attention when the little witch approached, her eyes wide and a small knowing smile on her face. Why did she get the feeling the woman knew something that she didn't?

She looked Tala up and down, then stuck out her hand. "I'm Lyra Magice."

Tala took it in hers. "Tala Channing."

Lyra held on a little too long. Tala got the notion the witch was testing her for some reason. Tingles of something swept over her arm. After a long pause, Lyra squeezed her hand and let go.

"Now that the niceties are over, we can get to work." Lyra grabbed her kit and made her way through the living room and out into the hall toward the front door without another word to anyone.

Flustered, Tala glanced around the room at the others.

Everyone was staring at her. Some of the officers had smug smiles on their faces. She suspected they knew she'd been transferred from the narcotics division as a form of punishment. It didn't matter to them that there was no proof to the allegations being tossed around the department like wads of useless paper.

Anger flowed over her and she turned her gaze from them, settling it on Caine. He was studying her with one perfect eyebrow raised.

"Don't let Jace and Lyra rattle you. They're not nearly as scary as they seem."

"Are you trying to say that their bark is worse than their bite?"

"Hell, no. I'd be lying, then." He smiled, his fangs winking at her in jest.

Ignoring the urge to return his smile, Tala straightened her shoulders, raised her chin and walked out of the room in the wake of her new charges.

She knew she had her work cut out for her. The Otherworlders were obviously not going to make it easy. But she'd never backed down from a fight before and she wasn't about to start.

Chapter 4

"Y ou're okay, right?"

Jace snarled at Lyra again as he prepared the piece of wax-imprinted wood for shoe-print scanning. This was the third time she'd asked him that question in the past hour and he was tired of answering.

"Would you quit asking me that?" He spun the wood around to get a better angle for the machine. "I said I'm fine."

As she leaned over his shoulder, he could see her pert little nose scrunch up. She was thinking about something. "It's just that I've never seen you incapacitated before."

Straightening, he reached over and pressed the switch on the scanning machine. "I wasn't incapacitated."

The machine's metal arm with mounted laser swiveled around and passed over the square of wood. The infrared light was taking a picture of the black wax shoe print. He hoped it would give them a lead. If not, at least it would give them the type of shoes the killer wore. Hiking boots, running shoes, loafers, each could tell them something about who they were after.

"Jace, you were on your knees trying to breathe." She snorted. "You were out of it, my friend."

"Yeah, well, I'm fine now," he told her without making eye contact. He didn't want her to see how on edge he truly was.

When he had exited the house and walked out into the dark of the early morning, he thought the sensation would abate. It had for a while. But the sight of the full moon cascading her glorious moonlight on him only ignited new sensations, a new itch.

He had sifted through the ashes in the metal drum and found a swatch of denim, a partial zipper and one half-charred red pump. No purse or ID to identify the victim, but maybe an idea of what she had worn the night she died. It would help build a picture of the murder. Just like all the other evidence.

By the time he had finished and piled into the SUV, his nerves were as jumpy as his pulse. His blood raced through his veins like liquid heat. He had to dig his nails into the palms of his hands to stop from shifting.

It was becoming progressively harder each passing moment.

And being cooped up inside like a prisoner didn't help matters, either. The lab was starting to feel like a cage.

Having a warden didn't help matters any.

His gaze shifted to the door of the analysis room they were in. Their police escort, Tala Channing, stood just outside the room, drinking coffee. There was something about her that bothered him. Something that wasn't quite right. And he couldn't put his finger on it.

When he had been collecting the evidence in the backyard, she had stood guard near the fence watching him. He felt her gaze on him like a physical thing. It had given him shivers and he was still having a hard time shaking them.

Her gaze lifted and for a brief moment their eyes met. A zing of something explosive flashed through the air between them. It hit him right between the eyes, pushing him back a step and into the worktable. Fumbling for something to hold, Jace pulled his gaze and forced it back onto his work.

What was going on? He'd never had that kind of reaction to anyone before, especially not a human.

A tap on his shoulder had him swinging around, a growl building in his throat.

Lyra stood staring at him, her eyes wide.

"What?" he barked.

"I've been talking to you for the past two minutes. You haven't heard a word I've said."

"I'm working. You know better than to interrupt me when I'm in the groove."

"You're in something, but I don't think it's a groove."

Ignoring Lyra, Jace tried to concentrate on the task at hand. The machine had finished scanning his print and he was now looking at a full image of it on the computer screen. It was a pretty good lift. From the picture he could make out several unique lines without the aid of the computer analysis. Now, he'd just have to put it into the computer system and see if it would be enough to run against the catalog of shoe treads on file. Hopefully, after a few hours they would get a match. And with it, a path to investigate.

The longer the case moved on without a suspect, the harder it would become for them to solve it. He didn't think they'd have much leeway on this one. He could just imagine the pressure Caine was receiving to solve this quickly and quietly.

They had been lucky with Lillian Crawford's case. The outside pressure to solve that crime was lessened by the fact that the human press and politicians wouldn't come into Necropolis. They had sent in Eve to work with them instead. And it proved to be a good move in the end. They had solved the case together—or thought they had.

Moving over to the keyboard, Jace started to punch in some commands. The computer remained quiet, unresponsive. He punched in the codes again. Still nothing. Frustration flowed through him; he banged on the keyboard.

"What's wrong with this thing?"

Lyra sidled up next to him, nudging him out of the

way. "Probably nothing wrong with the computer. It's the user that has issues."

He watched as she punched in the same commands he had. It didn't work for her, either. That gave him a small sense of satisfaction.

"Shoot, it's not working."

He gave her a sideways glare.

She ignored him and looked around the room. They had been alone for the better part of an hour. The lab tech had shown them the equipment then had skittered off as fast as he could. Jace had smelled the ripe stench of fear on the guy.

"Hey, Tala," Lyra called.

Tala flinched and looked up from staring at the floor.

Jace snarled. "Damn it, don't call her."

"Why ever not? She probably knows how to work this stupid system." Lyra waved at Tala, indicating for her to come into the room.

Jace watched out of the corner of his eye as the woman hesitated, glanced his way, then cautiously stepped into the room.

"Can I help you with something?" she asked.

There was something about her voice that caused the hair on his arms and legs to stand at attention. He could feel them rise even under his lab coat and his denim jeans. Clenching his teeth, he ran his hands down both sleeves.

Lyra pointed to the computer. "Do you know how to get into the system? We need to run this shoe print through the catalog."

With a half smile on her face, Tala walked around the counter to stand in front of the keyboard. Jace noticed how graceful she was when she moved. Unfortunately, he also noticed how well her khaki pants fit around her legs and rear end.

With apparent ease, her fingers raced over the keyboard and the partial print was transferred into the system. On-screen, Jace could see that the search had started.

She stood back and smiled. "There you are."

"Thank you, Tala." Lyra swung around and smirked at Jace. "You see, Jace, she's not useless."

Tala swiveled around and glowered at him. Whoa! It felt like he'd been hit by a tree trunk right across the head. He felt the need to take a step backward in retreat.

"You said what?" she demanded.

Jace put his hand up in defense and took a distancing step away. "Hey, I didn't say anything like that."

"What did you say then?" Her brow arched in question. Although she looked angry, Jace found he couldn't tear his gaze away. There was something so appealing about the woman. It wasn't that she was gorgeous, because she wasn't.

Her eyes were certainly stunning, a green reminiscent of fresh spring days. Her face and nose were thin, almost too thin, as was her body. *Willowy* would be what some would call her, he guessed. Long legs, slim hips, high pert breasts. She had a model's figure, not that Jace was complaining.

Her cheeks were flushed as she continued to glower

at him and her lips were slightly parted. He wondered
what she would do if he suddenly took her in his arms
and kissed her.

The urge to do so jolted through his system. It took
everything he had not to cross the distance between
them and satisfy his growing hunger. Damn it! He
wished he had mated before he came to San Antonio.
Why did he have to get the call from the lab right
before tussling with one of the pack females? Life just
wasn't fair.

Shaking his head to dislodge the unwanted erotic
notions racing through his mind, Jace glared at Lyra. "I
didn't say anything about you. The witch is a trouble-
maker."

"I am not." Lyra stuck out her lower lip in a pout, but
Jace could see the twinkle in her eye. She was pur-
posely pitting him and Tala against each other. Egging
on the tension between them.

He wondered if Lyra felt it as fiercely as he did. It
was so strong it was almost palpable.

"Are you still trying to get back at me for putting that
snake in your boot last summer?" he asked Lyra.

"No. Don't be an idiot."

"Oh, I'm an idiot now, am I?"

Lyra smirked. "Jace, you're *always* an idiot. You
can't even see what's in front of your face."

What did she mean by that? Before he could ask,
Caine walked into the room with Eve and Hector trailing
behind him.

He looked from Lyra to Jace to Tala and back to Jace. "I see everything's as normal as ever."

Lyra smiled innocently and turned toward Caine. "Tala was just showing us how to work the computer system so we could check for matching shoe treads."

Jace watched as Caine took thorough stock of Tala. He took a step forward, intent on protecting her from the vampire's gaze. But he stopped himself before he could move any further. What was with him? The predatory urge to protect Tala surged through him. Foolish to say the least, but the sensation would not go away, even when Caine turned that steely gaze onto him. Something was up. Jace could see concern in Caine's eyes.

"We have, yet again, a big problem."

"What else is new," Jace grunted.

"We got an ID on the victim." Caine ran a hand over his face. "It turns out she's Samantha Kipfer, the only daughter of Andrew Kipfer, a local television personality."

Jace cursed vehemently.

Caine nodded. "Well put, Jace. That's exactly how I feel right now." He leaned against the counter and crossed his arms. "So, be warned that the press is going to be all over this case. If we go out, we have to make sure there is local law enforcement with us at all times. The last thing any of us needs is more scrutiny."

Hector cleared his throat and looked at Tala. "I'll need you to stick to Lyra and Jace as much as you can, Channing. If they go out, you're going, too. To the crime scene, to the hotel, to a restaurant. Wherever. Your job is to keep the press away from them. Got me?"

Tala's gaze locked onto Jace. Heat instantly surged through his body. It was getting mighty uncomfortable in his jeans. Lord help him if he got an erection here and now. Talk about bad timing.

But the intensity of her stare made him quiver all over. She had power, this female. He had no clue why it affected him or how she possessed it. She smelled like Other, but he knew her not to be. It was an oddity and he wasn't sure if he was equipped to deal with it.

"I got you, sir," she said at last, then dropped her gaze.

"Take a couple of hours. Go home, get showered, eat and be back here ready to go fourteen hours if need be."

With a curt nod, she turned on her heel and marched out of the analysis room.

Sighing, Jace closed his eyes and ran a shaky hand through his mop of hair. This case was getting tougher by the minute. And he wasn't talking about the crime. That could be solved, eventually, with hard work and careful analysis of the evidence. It was the mystery of Tala Channing that piqued his interest. Who was she? And why did he want her so bad that he would drop to his knees in submission to have her?

Chapter 5

Violent fury raged through him while he sat on the hard wooden chair and stared out the apartment window toward the pinkened San Antonio skyline. His entire body shook with it.

They were here. He could feel them close by. The stink of their Otherworlder flesh nearly made him keel over in revulsion. To think he had spent so many years around them without doing just that.

Caine and his team of miscreants were in San Antonio trying to make sense of the latest murder. He smiled, worrying his fangs against his bottom lip. He was confident that they would never figure it out. They were too stupid and he was much too smart.

He'd been doing this for longer than most of them had been alive.

They had thought they had caught their killer. Using Mel Howard had been a fantastic ruse. The vampire had been greedy and pliable, eager to please someone he knew to be his master. The perfect pawn in his ongoing game.

Caine and his team had fallen for it beautifully. Like a movie being played out, perfectly scripted and brilliantly acted.

And he was the director.

Low mewls broke into his thoughts, disturbing him. Annoyed, he glanced over his shoulder at the queen-size bed in the middle of the bedroom. Standing, he ambled toward the bed. He enjoyed the way his naked body glistened with crimson streaks even in the soft light made by the black candles lit around the room.

As he neared, the young woman bound to the mattress began to whimper under her gag. He could smell her terror. It was a fragrant bouquet, making him drool with hunger.

He touched her foot and ran his long nails up to her ankle, where the rope he used to bind her dug cruelly into her sweet, pale flesh. Running his forefinger over the restraints, he gathered the blood and skin shed there onto the pad of his finger. He brought it up to his mouth and sucked it between his lips. Such sweet honey.

Taking a step away from the bed, he studied his work. A network of crisscrossing red marks lined her body. He had spent hours on her. Every cut took several seconds to complete and he had reveled in the way she had squirmed and whimpered in agony.

The girl had been an easy mark. So easily charmed and seduced. He had picked her out in a club. Plied her with drinks and compliments, then accepted her invitation up to her apartment. Silly girl had no clue exactly what she had been inviting into her bed.

She knew now.

By the way she stared at him in utter horror, she knew exactly what he was and where he'd come from.

He trailed his talon over her torso to her breast. She tried to draw back from his touch, but she had nowhere to go. He chuckled at her instinctive response.

She was going to make a lovely present for Caine and his team.

"You're going to die, my dear," he chimed in a sing-song voice. "And it's going to be brutal and painful."

Chapter 6

Tala unbuttoned her white blouse, shrugged it off and tossed it into the hamper in the corner of her bedroom. Walking to her closet, she grabbed an identical shirt. As she slipped it on and started buttoning it, she wandered out of her bedroom and into the kitchen.

She thanked whatever benevolent spirit had allowed her a few hours to come home and recharge. Being in the lab had been stifling. She had tried hard not to be in the same room as Jace. She volunteered to get coffee, run to the various labs, be the go-between, anything to keep her out of the same space as the lycan. It had been working up until Lyra had called her in to run the computer.

Although Tala had only been in the room with him

for no more than fifteen minutes, she could still feel the electrical current that had been zinging through the air between them skimming across her skin. She'd never felt anything like it before. And she didn't want to feel it ever again.

He was off-limits.

She shouldn't even have been thinking about him, especially in such sensual ways. It was far too dangerous. Even though everything about him screamed sex and seduction, she had to force herself to stay away. Of course, that was going to be nearly impossible since Hector had assigned her as Jace and Lyra's police escort. Why couldn't she have gotten the vampire and his human wife? She had no fear of them.

Opening the refrigerator door, Tala took out leftover Chinese food and a jug of milk. She opened the small white box and dug in. Between bites, she chugged from the milk carton.

While she stood in the kitchen leaning against the counter to eat, she turned on the small TV that sat in the little nook separating the kitchen from the living room. She flipped the channels until she got to the news. The sheriff was giving a press conference about the murder.

Andrew Kipfer was a much-loved local celebrity and Tala knew the city was mourning with him for the loss of his only daughter, Samantha. She had been only twenty.

Tala remembered seeing her once at a charity fund-raiser a few years ago. She had been a sweet, innocent-looking girl, blond, blue-eyed, perky and upbeat. A good girl with good, upstanding friends.

Tala certainly knew that bad things happened to decent people. She'd worked in the narcotics division long enough to learn that lesson well. But how did a girl like Samantha end up in a dilapidated house, hanging upside down from the rafters with her throat slit?

Suddenly, a jolt of pain shot down Tala's arm to her hand. Clenching her fist, she crushed the Chinese food box. Noodles and sauce oozed out from the cardboard around her fingers and dripped onto the floor.

She swung around and dumped the box and contents into the sink. She turned on the tap and washed off the remains of her breakfast. Closing her eyes, she bit out a curse. The pain was coming too soon. She thought she'd have another couple days for sure before she'd need to take care of it.

It was being around Jace that spurned the increase and speed of her cycle. Her body was reacting to him. It called to him just like she had read it would.

Twisting the water off, Tala grabbed the dish towel to dry her hands and walked out of the kitchen, down the hall and into the bathroom. After tossing the towel on the vanity, she opened her medicine cabinet.

There were the usual items lining the shelves. Headache pills, antacids, vitamins, old prescription drugs. In the top corner on the top shelf was a bottle of unassuming eyedrops.

She took down the plastic container, titled her head

back and opened her eyes wide. Holding it above her, she squeezed a drop of liquid into each eye. Pain, sharp and immediate, radiated over her.

She wanted to scream as liquid fire shot through her system. Tearing, ripping agony surged over her. It started in her eyes and raced from the top of her head to the tips of her big toes. It was the same every time. And every time she felt like dying.

Dropping the container into the sink, she shuffled sideways to find the toilet and sat down on the closed lid. Her legs were shaking too much to support her weight. Clamping her eyes shut to stem the tears, she buried her head in her hands and rode it out.

It was for the best, she told herself. She muttered that under her breath repeatedly until the adrenaline rush ended and the pain subsided to a dull ache.

When she was able to control her breathing again, she stood and went about cleaning up the mess. After everything was put away, she splashed cold water on her face and glanced in the mirror.

You're okay, Tala. You're a survivor.

After running a comb through her hair and applying a thin layer of lip gloss, Tala figured she was ready to go. She looked in control and that was all that mattered.

She left the bathroom and went into her living room to put on her shoes, her gun holster and her jacket. Once she had her holster on and was buckling it up, her phone rang. Not her cell phone but her home phone.

She hesitated to answer. There was likely only one

person on the other end and Tala didn't really want to talk to her today. But loyalty needled her and she snatched the phone on its sixth ring.

"I thought maybe you weren't home," her mother, Claudia, whined.

"I'm on the way out, Mother. Is there something you needed?"

"A mother can't call her only child to see how she's doing?"

Tala's temples started to throb. It wouldn't be long before she got a migraine. Her mother had the uncanny ability to bring one on instantly.

"I just saw you on Sunday, Mother. Everything was fine then and everything is fine now."

"Are you sure? I have a feeling that something is going on."

"Nothing's going on. I'm just doing my job as usual and coming home alone, as usual." Tala couldn't keep the sarcasm out of her voice. She was getting tired of having the same conversations with her mother every week. Tired of supplying the same excuses.

"A mother knows, Tala." She paused and Tala swore she could hear the woman's brain grinding gears. "Are you stressed? If you are, you have to remember to increase your doses."

Tala wanted to scream at her. To rant and rage about what she just put herself through. That her mother had no clue the pain and suffering she endured day after day. And that it was all her mother's fault.

But she held her tongue. As usual.

"I told you law enforcement was the wrong career for you, Tala. You need to do something less stressful with your life. I thought you liked working at the bank."

"I hated that job. It was boring."

"Oh, Tala, you're too restless. You hardly gave it a chance. You only worked there for three years. Hardly enough time to let it grow on you."

"Mom, I have to go."

She could tell instantly that her mother was crying.

"I worry about you, my darling." She sniffed. "I did my best by you. It was so hard."

"I know, Mom. I know." Tala sighed. Guilt always worked on her. Her mom had been using it since Tala had reached puberty. "I've got to go. I'll phone you when I can."

She set the phone back in its cradle and slumped down into the big easy chair, pressing her fingers to her right temple. The last thing she needed was to get more uptight. Already she was teetering on a precarious edge. One more push and Tala was sure to drop off. Where she ended up would most likely not be a good place. Not for her, not for anyone around her.

Thank goodness Claudia didn't know about the case. And especially about Jace. She was sure the woman would lose all sense of reality and do something crazy. Like the last time, when Tala had been only twelve years old and blossoming into a teenager.

Shaking the thoughts of her past, Tala took in a few

deep breaths, stood and rotated her shoulders to ease the tension solidifying there. She needed to be cool and calm. She needed to keep her wits about her.

She needed to stay away from Jace Jericho.

But what she needed and what she was going to get were always two entirely different things. That was something she learned a long time ago. Something she'd been living with for thirteen years. And she knew it wasn't going to change anytime soon, no matter how much she needed it to.

Chapter 7

Jace watched Caine pace at the front of the conference room and knew the chief was feeling the pressure. To an untrained eye, the vampire appeared to be as collected and aloof as usual. But Jace could see the slight twitch at Caine's jaw and smell his frustration.

It wasn't a normal odor, something akin to turpentine. Over the years, Jace had learned to identify it for what it was. He could count on one hand how many times he'd detected it on Caine, which said a lot.

"Okay, let's go over what is similar to Lillian Crawford's murder and what is different. The differences here I think will be the key in solving this one."

Caine looked around the room and at every member

of the team. Hector, along with Rick, one of the lab techs, joined Jace, Lyra and Eve around the rectangular conference table. Jace was surprised at the level of professionalism coming from the human captain. Maybe the entire human population of San Antonio weren't useless. But he'd reserve his final verdict until after this case was closed.

Caine opened the file on the table in front of him. He gathered the autopsy pictures and spread them around the table. The grisly images of the victim's dead body flashed like sickly pale light on the dark mahogany surface.

"Samantha Kipfer died from exsanguination. Her neck was opened from left to right, which indicates a right-handed killer. Her blood was taken from the scene, hence no blood pool. And her body was painted in her own blood with magical symbols, indicative of a demon summoning." He paused and glanced around the room. "That is what is the same. Now the differences. Her throat was slashed open with a claw and not a knife. She was not raped. There was no semen present or vaginal trauma. There were no bite marks. She was drugged, but not with Vampatamine or Heparin. She had trace amounts of MDMA in her system."

"Ecstasy?" Eve asked.

Caine nodded. "So, from this, what can we determine?"

"That we're looking for a human killer," Jace remarked.

Rick cleared his throat. "How can you be so sure? Her throat was clawed open, not cut."

"Because if it had been a vampire, she would've been

bitten. He or she wouldn't have been able to help themselves." Jace smiled without humor. "And if it had been a lycan, she would've been gutted." He lifted his hand and forced the shift. His nails grew into sharp curved claws. "He or she wouldn't be able to help themselves."

Lyra elbowed him in the side and whispered, "Jerk."

"Jace." Caine chastised. "Let's keep our claws and teeth to ourselves on this case, all right?"

Wriggling his fingers at Rick, Jace pushed the change back and his nails began to recede into his fingers. Pain ripped through his arms, but he kept his face calm. "Right you are there, Chief."

Rick forced his gaze away from Jace and set it on Lyra. "What about witches? The demon summoning is a witch thing, isn't it?"

This time it was Lyra's turn to look aghast. "I don't think so. It's totally against our nature to kill. A demon summoning could be anyone."

Hector shuffled in his chair, pushing it back a little from the table. Jace could tell he was growing agitated. His scent was one of nervous anticipation. "Let's move on with the evidence, please."

"Hector's right. We have to follow the trail that's been left. Not make rash decisions without having all the questions answered," Caine added. He turned to Eve, who sat on his right. "What did the witness have to say?"

"Not much. She said she didn't see anything but the body hanging from the ceiling. She doesn't recall seeing anyone else there or any vehicles in the area."

Eve shook her head. "I don't think the girl would even remember her own car if she had driven there. She was out of it. Big-time junkie. She had track marks all over her arms and legs."

"Speaking of drugs," Lyra offered. "Maybe we should follow the Ecstasy. That's a designer drug, right? Used at raves and the like? Maybe Samantha is involved in that culture."

Caine nodded. "We need to get into her house and search her room. If she's a regular user, she'll have a stash somewhere, I'm sure."

"Tala can be of help on this," Hector piped in. "She used to work in the narcotics division. She's done extensive information-collection on the various drugs being used in the city. She knows who's dealing and where."

"Excellent. She can work with Jace and Lyra instead of just escorting them around."

Jace felt his stomach flip over. He didn't want Tala to work with him. He was having a difficult time as it was just looking at her, let alone being around her. Being able to smell her and feel the heat of her body was going to pose a big problem.

Jace lifted his hand. "Are you sure that's a good idea? Having an inexperienced person on this case could prove to be a disaster."

Caine met his gaze. "I'm sure under your tutelage, Jace, she will do just fine." He shut the file he was holding, effectively ending the conversation. "Jace and Lyra, you are on the victim's residence. Hector, Eve and I are going back to Lillith's family and friends to see if there is a connection." Caine slid the file under his arm. "The lab is still working on the fiber and trace evidence we collected at the scene and on the body. There's got to be something we can go on." Nodding to each of them around the table, he added, "Okay, everyone keep in touch. We'll meet back here in a few hours to see where we are."

With that, Caine moved toward the door. Eve and Hector followed his lead. Once the door was open, Hector called in Tala.

She appeared in the doorway, looking fresh-faced and eager. But Jace noticed something else about her. There was something off or missing about her now. He couldn't place it. Was she wearing glasses before? He couldn't recall.

Whatever it was it had changed her.

"You'll be working with Jace and Lyra at the Kipfer residence. You do as they instruct, okay?" Hector said.

She nodded, but didn't meet Hector's gaze. Instead her eyes fastened on Jace. He could feel her attention, piercing his body, dissecting his soul. Why did she affect him so much?

Chapter 8

The crowd of reporters swarming in front of the Kipfer residence was astonishing. Jace could feel the intense press of their bodies even from the sanctity of the back-seat of the crime lab's vehicle. It was as if the metal of the doors were bending under the strain, reaching toward him, trying to touch him. A cold sweat broke out over his body. Clenching his hands into tight fists, he swallowed down the rising panic.

As Tala inched the SUV through the mass of people, she cursed under her breath at the swarm. Jace's lips twitched a few times at the words she sputtered. It still didn't stop the reporters from banging on the windows with their microphones, screaming for sound bites, anything to quench the thirst of the media horde.

The only bite Jace wanted to give them was one on their collective butts. He'd call them all blood-sucking vampires, but that would be a grave insult to all the vampires he knew.

Once they were through the crowd outside the Kipfer estate, they parked the vehicle, jumped out and grabbed their respective kits. The pressure he was feeling instantly released the moment Jace stepped out into the clean crisp air. He let out the breath he hadn't realized he had been holding and followed Lyra and Tala into the Kipfer house.

They assembled just outside of the victim's bedroom. The girl's parents were in the kitchen talking with a detective who had arrived earlier. They had already given their permission to the crime-scene unit to thoroughly look through Samantha's room and to take what they needed.

Lyra peered through the open doorway. "Good thing she's got a big room. Or the three of us would be glued together." She smirked at Jace while snapping on her latex gloves. Picking up her kit, she walked into the room, leaving Jace and Tala to themselves.

Jace took out two sets of gloves from his kit. He handed a pair to Tala. "Have you ever been on a crime scene before?"

"Not counting yesterday?"

"Yes."

"Then twice. Once during basic training and another time after a drug bust."

Crouching next to his kit, Jace took out several numbered yellow-plastic markers and handed them to Tala. "Just follow the same protocol. If you see anything out of the ordinary or something you think needs a second look, set one of these markers beside it."

"I think I can handle it." After snapping on her gloves, she brushed past Jace and into the room.

Taking in a deep breath, Jace wondered what he ever did to deserve being shackled to Tala. She was even snarlier than he was. If that were possible.

He put on his own gloves and followed the ladies into the room.

The room was typical of a young woman used to the benefits of growing up with money, Jace thought. Everything was neat, orderly and professionally decorated. Her bed was expertly made with powder-blue blankets hanging down to the pristine beige carpet. Cream throw pillows were artfully arranged against the headboard.

"Do you think she cleans her own room?" Jace asked as he surveyed the room. "The bed looks too done up. I wonder if the maid has cleaned the room since the girl's disappearance."

Lyra glanced up at him from inspecting the dresser drawers. "That's a good question. I'll go ask." She promptly left the room to search for the answer.

While Jace examined the area around the bed, he watched Tala out of the corner of his eye. She had started her search in the farthest corner of the room, a reading nook of sorts, complete with a built-in bench along the window. It was a good place to start. One he would've picked himself if she hadn't beaten him to it.

While he waited to hear back from Lyra, Jace got on his hands and knees and checked under the bed. He found a bag shoved to the middle. Reaching, he grabbed it and dragged it forward. Once in the light, he could see that it was a black-leather gym bag.

He unzipped it. Inside were a sports bra, cotton shorts, socks, running shoes and a Louis Vuitton compact makeup bag. Jace reached in and took out the makeup bag. When he opened it, a plastic ID card fell out onto the rug. He picked it up.

"Looks like she worked out at Hard Bodies Health Spa." Setting the card down, he continued to search the bag.

"Beats me why people insist on working out indoors with a hundred other people, when all they have to do is put on some good sneakers, step outside their door and start running."

Nodding, Jace glanced over at her. "I hear that. I'd rather go for a long run any day."

"I do three miles every day," she commented off-handedly as she set a plastic card onto the window sill. "I got prints on the window."

Jace did a slow perusal of her body from toe to head. She definitely had a runner's body. Long and lean. He bet she had exquisitely shaped thighs and calves.

As he continued to watch her, he pictured her in a tank top and shorts, her auburn hair bobbing up and down in a ponytail as she sprinted up a path much like the one on Silent Hill in Necropolis that he ran whenever he could get away. He could see the way her muscles would bunch as she ran, the way her sweat would trickle down her back and chest. With a clarity that almost startled him, he imagined the sweat trail traveling down her neck, in between her pert breasts and pooling inside her navel.

Licking his lips, he thought about dipping his tongue right in that spot and then trailing it lower still….

"I'd say you found some flake."

Blinking, Jace shook his head and stared at Tala. "Excuse me?"

She pointed to his hand. "The lip gloss container you're holding, it's full of cocaine."

Jace looked down at the cylindrical tube he'd been holding while fantasizing about Tala. When he held it up, he could see a white powder inside. Unscrewing the lid, he pulled out the lip applicator. The tip was covered in a snow-white substance.

He slid it back into the container and screwed it on. Jace looked at Tala as she continued to search through the victim's books near the window. "How did you know?"

She shrugged. "I worked drug intel for a couple of years. I know how people hide drugs. Their ingeniousness and stupidity are limitless."

"No, I mean how could you see it from over there?" Eyeing her still, he slid the lip gloss into an evidence bag. He could smell her anxiety and taste it on his tongue like smoke from a fire.

She wouldn't meet his gaze. "I have great eyesight."

Jace set the gym bag aside, slid the evidence into his kit and wandered over to where Tala was inspecting one of three stuffed bears sitting daintily on the bench along the window's ledge.

He noticed the way her body quivered when he stepped in next to her. His muscles were doing the same thing. Being near her was like stepping out into an electrical storm with lightning flashing across the sky and striking the ground a mere foot away. Exhilarated and powerful. That's how he felt around her.

Concentrate on work. Work is safe.

Taking up his camera, he took several shots of the things Tala had indicated with the yellow markers. Fingerprints on the window. Likely the victim's, but because the window opened onto a ledge that could easily be accessed from the large tree next to it, he would lift the prints. Maybe she was abducted from her room. Or she left that way of her own accord. Sneaking out at night to rendezvous with a secret lover. Or worse.

Going back to his kit to grab the black dusting powder, a brush and a lift card, Jace noticed that Tala waved the stuffed bear in front of her face. If he didn't know better, he'd swear she was scenting the toy. Which was a ridiculous notion, but one he wasn't able to dismiss out of hand.

He came back with his equipment and dusted the fingerprint while Tala inspected another of the little bears. This one was white with a bright pink dress. Before Jace could react, she ripped its head off and was tearing out its stuffing.

"What are you looking for?" he asked.

Ignoring him, she continued to pull out white cotton batting. Digging in with her fingers, she came away with a clear plastic bag. She dropped the bear and held up the bag to Jace.

"Show me the love." She smiled. Inside the bag were a handful of small blue pills with panda bears stamped on them. "MDMA, Ecstasy, XTC, whatever you want to call it. She was definitely a regular user."

"Damn."

She set them down on the bench next to the decapitated bear so Jace could photograph it. "I once found heroine in a baby's diaper while the baby was wearing it. Nothing surprises me anymore."

After taking several photos, Jace went to his kit and grabbed a big evidence bag and shoved the pills and the headless bear into it, sealing it shut.

"Good catch," he commented.

Without looking up from her inspection of the other bear, she nodded. "Thanks."

He could sense her pleasure at his words.

"How did you know?"

She shrugged. "Like I said, years of knowledge of how drug users and abusers function."

She was lying. He could tell instantly. He didn't

know how he knew, but he knew. There was something about the way her eyes shifted and the sound of her heartbeat that gave her away. He wanted to press her, but decided this wasn't the best time. It was obvious she had her secrets. And who was he to pry them out of her?

"Okay, what can the pills tell us? Anything?"

"The pills can't, but I can. I know who the players are that deal blue pandas and where they deal." She gave him a half smile. "I just need to talk to my contact at narc and confirm."

He liked her mouth. Full and sensuous. Kissable. An urge to lean over and press his lips to hers settled over him. He felt drawn to her. Like a bee to delicious honey.

She caught his gaze and her cheeks reddened. He wondered if she could sense his attraction to her.

Instead of grabbing her and crushing his mouth to hers, he took a step back and nodded. "That's cool. That's more than we had before."

Thankfully, Lyra took that moment to bounce into the room. "Guess what? The maid did clean the room a day ago. Samantha hasn't been home since yesterday morning."

"We need to retrace her steps," Jace said as he moved back to the bed and picked up the gym bag. "I think this Hard Bodies gym is the perfect place to start. I bet she was there yesterday. With a shape like hers, she definitely worked out every day."

"Anything else interesting?" Lyra asked as she continued to rummage through the victim's dresser drawers.

"Tala found a bag of ecstasy in one of the vic's stuffed bears," Jace informed her.

Lyra glanced over her shoulder at Tala and smiled. "Wow, you're a regular little police dog, aren't you?"

"Why would you say that?" Jace and Tala demanded in unison.

Lyra glanced from Tala to Jace then back to Tala, with her eyebrow arched in obvious curiosity. "Ah, no offense. I meant it as a compliment, as Jace knows very well." She trained her intense gaze onto Jace.

He knew she was probing him and the situation. There was that sibling thing in play. The witch knew him inside and out. By the twitch of her lips, she could probably sense his growing attraction to Tala. If Lyra hadn't sensed it before, his outburst in Tala's defense had just made it clear.

He had to watch himself. If he wasn't careful he was going to start marking his territory. He wondered if Tala had any idea how lycans worked. If she did, she'd be running for the hills and he would have no choice but to chase her.

Tala shook her head. "No offense taken. The comment just took me off guard. I'm not usually compared to a dog."

"You're lucky. I get it all the time," Jace scoffed.

Lyra started to laugh. And it wasn't long before Tala's resolve broke and she was laughing, too. Jace looked from one woman to the other and couldn't help the laughter from bubbling up to the surface, either.

In a matter of minutes, the three of them were doubled over in laughter. Tears streamed down Lyra's face.

Jace's comment hadn't been that funny, but it certainly relieved the growing tension in the room and between the three of them. Something that had definitely needed to be alleviated before it got too serious.

When their laughter had died, Jace straightened and ran a hand over his mouth. "Okay, let's finish up this scene here and go on over to the gym to see what we can dig up." He took out his cell phone. "I'll call Caine to let him know what we're doing, see what he thinks. But I have a feeling we're on the right trail."

As he dialed, Jace locked eyes with Tala. She was staring at him, the green in her eyes seeming to glow. If he didn't know better, he'd say she was tagging him, letting him know that she was interested in having him court her.

The only thing was, it was a purely lycan thing to do.

Chapter 9

Tala didn't know what had happened at the Kipfer house inside the victim's room, but something had transpired between her and Jace. Somehow she felt connected to him. In a way she'd never experienced with anyone else. Not even her mother.

She could now tell when he was thinking about her. It sizzled over her skin like static electricity, a foreign sensation. One she wasn't sure if she hated or liked, a lot.

Tala sensed Jace watching her as the three of them walked into Hard Bodies. She looked over her shoulder and caught him. It was easy to read the feral look in his eyes. Hunger. Need. Unsure what to do, Tala returned his stare. At least Jace had the decency to look embarrassed. He quickly turned his gaze to the other people entering the facility.

Putting a hand to her thumping chest, Tala wasn't sure if she could handle him looking at her like that more than once. His look was heated and intense. It carried weight and substance. As if he could actually stroke her with its intensity alone. The thought had her licking her lips. She knew instinctively his touch would be wild and feral, possessive even.

And she ached for it like nothing before.

When they reached the front desk of the fitness club, Jace took the lead and stepped up to the counter.

The enthusiastic young woman at the counter beamed at him. "Hi, I'm April. Please tell me how I can help you today."

Tala couldn't help but notice that the girl's obvious silicone breasts beamed at Jace, too.

"Well, April, you can tell me if you recognize this girl." Jace flashed the gym ID card to her.

She glanced down at it then back to Jace, her smile still glued to her tanned face. "Of course, that's Sam. She's a regular here."

"Was she here yesterday?"

April's gaze flickered from Jace to Tala and Lyra then back to Jace. "Um, are you a cop or something?"

Jace shook his head. "No, nothing as boring as that. I'm with the crime lab."

"Oh, that's so cool." She batted her eyelashes at him.

Tala nearly groaned at the overindulgent flirtation.

"I didn't see her, but I can sure check the register for you to see if she was."

Jace smiled at her. "That would be great, April."

As the perky redhead bounced over to the computer to check the registry, Jace leaned over the counter and eyed the girl's rear end in her tight Lycra shorts. Tala smirked at his leering. At least, that was what she considered it. The man had no couth. Hadn't he, just moments ago, been staring at her assets? It wasn't like she was jealous or anything. She just thought it was rude. Despite her rather violent urge to jump on the bouncy April and eliminate her from the equation, Tala still didn't consider herself jealous.

Turning her lethal stare away from Jace, Tala caught Lyra grinning at her. "What?" she barked.

Lyra shook her head, but kept on smiling. "Nothing."

April bounced back to the counter and batted her eyelashes at Jace. "Yup, Sam was here yesterday in the afternoon, around two o'clock."

"Does she train with anyone in particular?"

April nodded. "Rock."

"The guy's name is Rock?" Jace asked.

"His real name is Darryl Rockland. But we all call him Rock, because, well, he's, like, hard as a rock." She giggled, then reached out and touched Jace on the arm.

Tala was just about ready to bite her own tongue clean off. She couldn't handle April's perky demeanor and the way she flirted with Jace any longer. Taking a step forward, Tala slapped her hand down on the counter. That definitely got everyone's attention.

"Where can we find Rock?" she demanded.

April's face fell and she almost looked like she was going to pout. "He's at the treadmills with another client." Tilting her head, she glared at Tala. "Who are you?"

Tala reached into her pants and pulled out her wallet. "I'm the cop." She flashed April her badge. "Does Samantha have a locker she uses here?"

April nodded, suddenly somber. "I can check for you."

"You do that."

When the girl wandered back to the computer, Jace growled at her. "What was that all about?"

"Getting our job done."

"What do you think I'm doing?"

She cocked her hip and lifted her brow. "Trying to get a date."

"Not likely," he smirked. "I don't have to try anything. If I wanted that girl, she'd be mine." He snapped his fingers. "Just like that."

"You arrogant son of a—"

"Excuse me?"

Both Tala and Jace whipped around to look at April. "What?" they growled in unison.

"She has locker number twenty-three."

While flashing her OCU credentials, Lyra pushed past both Tala and Jace and smiled at the girl. "Could you open that for me, April?"

The girl nodded and came around the counter to lead Lyra into the locker room. Lyra turned around and glared at Tala and Jace,

"Now, I'm going to go search her locker, you two behave and go find Rock." With a final shake of her head, Lyra followed April to Sam's locker.

Feeling admonished, Tala looked at Jace sheepishly. She was all set to apologize when he grunted, turned on his heel and marched into the fitness center. Gritting her teeth, she followed him. Arrogant jerk.

It didn't take much investigative work to find Rock. He was a rather large young man, tanned, shaved head, with a body that looked like stone. He was coaching a woman in her thirties on the treadmill. But Tala noticed that he was mostly eyeing the woman's jiggling breasts.

The guy didn't even so much as flinch when Tala and Jace approached him.

Tala flipped him her badge. "Darryl Rockland?"

As if coming out of a trance, Darryl slowly raised his head and met Tala's gaze. The man looked drugged.

"Rock," he stated. "Everyone calls me Rock."

Jace took a step forward and showed Darryl the victim's ID card. "Did you work out with Samantha Kipfer yesterday afternoon?"

Darryl didn't look at the card but continued to look at Jace. Tala could see a tic in the guy's jaw. Something was definitely wrong with him. He was on some kind of drug. She'd seen similar reactions in other long-time users.

"I might have," he answered, as he rubbed the palm of his hand on his leg as if he had an itch. "I'd have to check my logbook."

"You can't remember?"

"Hey dude, I have a lot of clients. And one day blurs into the next. To be positive, I'd have to check my logbook."

Jace stared him down, but Darryl wasn't flinching. "Okay, go check."

Without another word, Darryl turned toward his client and told her he'd be right back. Then he wandered through the gym to a door marked Employees Only.

Tala watched him carefully. She didn't like the feel of the situation. Something was off. It crawled over her skin like gooseflesh.

"He's going to run."

Jace frowned at her. "What?"

"I'm telling you, he's going to run. He's hiding something and he's making a run for it right now."

"How do you figure that?"

"I don't know." She shook her head, but kept his gaze. "I can just sense it."

Jace eyed her for a few moments, searching her face. He must have seen the one thing he was looking for, because he nodded and said, "Okay, let's go."

With Jace in the lead, they moved toward the employees-only door in the far corner of the gym. Jace grabbed the doorknob and jiggled it. It was locked. There was a keypad on the locking mechanism and only an employee would know the right code.

"Damn it. Now what?" Tala remarked.

Winking, Jace grabbed the door handle again and

squeezed. Tala heard the audible pop of the door lock snapping. She hoped no one else had.

"Anyone looking?" Jace asked.

Tala surveyed the room behind them. The various occupants were concentrating on lifting weights or counting steps on the stepper and not looking in their direction.

"It's clear."

Slowly, Jace opened the door, peered in and then stepped through. Tala followed him in so close she could hear his heart thumping. She wondered if hers was just as loud.

They were in a hallway that led to about four other rooms. Tala held her breath that they didn't run into anyone along the way that had brains enough to call their bluff. Even with her badge, she'd be hard pressed to give a reason for their presence. They didn't really have sufficient cause to check on Darryl, except for her bad feeling.

The first room on the left was a men's washroom. Pushing open the door, Jace listened for a moment then went in. Leaning against the wall, Tala tried to wait patiently. What she really wanted to do was rush in there and help out. She loved this part of police work. Chasing the bad guys. Her adrenaline was zinging through her system. The rush gave her a euphoric high. It was better than drugs any day. It was the reason she had gone into law enforcement.

After a couple of minutes, the door to the bathroom opened and Jace walked out. "It's clear." He nodded toward the next door—the woman's washroom. "Your turn."

Taking a deep breath, Tala swung open the door and walked in. There was no one at the sinks. She checked the three stalls to find them empty. She was almost disappointed that Darryl wasn't in there, hiding.

Doing one last sweep of the room, her eyes lifted up to the small window above the garbage can and feminine product dispensers. It was open. The glass pane swung outward. A black scuff mark marred the pristine white wall.

He'd gone out the window.

Her statement was confirmed when she heard metal—garbage cans maybe—crashing onto the cement.

"Jace!" she called. "He's running!"

Without waiting, Tala set her left foot on top of the garbage can, grabbed hold of the window ledge and pulled herself up. Once there, she was able to stick her head out the window. She saw Darryl running down the alley. She wiggled the rest of the way through, swung her right leg over and jumped down onto the ground.

In a matter of seconds she was chasing him.

Darryl was quick, but Tala had been running all her life. Her mother swore that Tala had been born with sneakers already glued to her feet.

Her long legs pumped like pistons. Her breath came in vigorous measured rasps. She knew how to put on the speed and keep it. So it wasn't long before she caught up to him.

When he reached the mouth of the alley, he glanced over his shoulder. His first big mistake. He lost his rhythm and momentum when he did that. Good thing for Tala, though. It gave her the opportunity to take him down.

Leaping, she wrapped her arms around his waist and pushed him back. He outweighed her by seventy pounds easy, but she had momentum, gravity and determination on her side. The bastard was going down. And hard.

Darryl landed on his side with Tala on top. Before she could maneuver around and get him into a submission hold, he grabbed her by the hair and yanked her off him. She rolled onto her back, but was scrambling to her feet before he could run again.

Except he didn't run. He was staring down at her with fury in his face. She probably looked like an easy mark to him: female, slender, a lot smaller than him.

Before she could gain her feet, he kicked her. Instinctively she bent her arms to protect her chest. He had thick meaty legs and his kick was something fierce. But she managed to block most of it with her forearms. Just the tip of his shoe managed to find a weak spot between her elbows and into her gut. The force of the blow sent her sprawling backward.

Her eyes teared up from the pain of the strike. Had he found a rib? From the agony that tore through her, Tala thought maybe he had. Rolling onto her other side, Tala brought her knees up to protect herself from the next kick she was sure was coming.

But it didn't come.

Through the tears, Tala could see Jace on Darryl. The lycan was behind Darryl and had both of Darryl's arms twisted and crossed behind his neck in a submission hold reminiscent of the WWE. Tala could also see that Jace's eyes smoldered like embers in a fire. The veins in his neck had popped and he looked very near to shifting.

Clutching her injured side, Tala gained her feet and approached Jace. This close, she could plainly see that his jaw had elongated and canines poked out between his lips. She could also see that Darryl was near unconsciousness. His eyes were rolling back into his sockets. She smelled the urine that stained his cotton shorts.

"Jace," she said, "Back down. You got him. He isn't going anywhere."

He met her gaze and she could see the rage flaring in his eyes. But she also discerned something else. Concern. Longing. Was it for her?

"He hurt you," he growled. And it was closer to a growl than not. But she understood him. Surprisingly so.

"I'm fine. Really." She lifted her arms and twisted back and forth to show him that she was all right. She tried to keep the pain that tore through from showing on her face. After lowering her arms, she touched him on the shoulder. "Let him go, Jace. We can't question him if he's out cold."

Underneath her palm, Tala could actually feel his body relax. The fire in his eyes dimmed and she watched in awe as his jaw receded into itself. It was mesmerizing to witness. She thought she'd be disturbed by Jace's ability to shift back and forth. Instead, she found herself intrigued and a little bit aroused.

Back to normal, Jace released his hold on Darryl. The fitness trainer slumped to the ground, incapacitated but still conscious.

Tala stood over Darryl. Reaching down, she handcuffed his hands behind his back then rolled him into a sit. "You're an idiot for running. You're going to have a headache for hours and I'm booking you for assault on a police officer."

As she read Darryl his Miranda rights, Tala was acutely aware of Jace's presence. He had moved closer to her, standing only a foot away, watching her. It was as if just being near her calmed him.

She had thought she would be angry by Jace's aggressive display. She didn't normally go for macho behavior. But with Jace, she found it endearing, soothing even. In the back of her mind, she felt protected and secure. Like nothing would hurt her again. Not with Jace Jericho around.

What she wasn't sure about was how she felt about that. On one hand it appeased her, like the comfort of family and home.

But it also scared the living hell out of her. So much that she didn't know what to do with it.

Chapter 10

Pacing the conference room, Jace was becoming stir-crazy. He'd been cooped up going on two hours now. Darryl was spouting off about police brutality and his lawyer was causing a stink. So the powers that be decided it would be a good idea if they caged Jace for a while to get him out of the way. Little did they know how much of a cage it seemed to Jace.

After he and Tala brought Darryl in for questioning, the guy lawyered up almost immediately. The only thing they did get out of him was that he did see and train Samantha Kipfer that day around two o'clock. She had been there for an hour. After that, he claimed he didn't know where she went.

Jace was certain the guy knew more than he was admitting. Darryl had a dishonest smell. Like sour milk.

Tala had also thought Darryl was keeping information to himself. In fact, as soon as Darryl screeched for a lawyer she excused herself to make some phone calls. She was certain that Darryl was Samantha's ecstasy dealer. She just needed to talk to her contacts in the narcotics division.

When Jace had asked how she knew, she told him she could smell it on Darryl. Considering the circumstances, Jace thought that was the strangest comment she'd ever made. Now, if he had said something like that, it would've made sense. His sense of smell was considerably heightened. He could discern twenty separate odors at once. A human didn't have that ability.

Tala was quickly becoming the most intriguing person Jace had ever met. She was guarded. A woman with secrets. But the cracks were starting to show in her walls and he was attracted to what he could glimpse in between.

The door to the conference room opened and Caine strode in, looking as polished and collected as ever. The only time he'd ever seen the vampire undone was the night Eve had been kidnapped from his house. It was in that moment, Jace truly understood how much Caine loved his human woman.

Not once had Jace ever thought he could like, let alone love, a human. But after meeting Tala and spending time with her, his resolve wasn't so steady and sure.

"I'm going nuts in here, Chief."

Caine sat on one of the chairs at the table and set his file folders down. "I know. It's absolutely ridiculous, the human bureaucracy, but we have to abide by it since we are on their turf, so to speak."

"How are we doing, anyway? Can we hold this guy as a suspect?"

"We have nothing to go on. The white fibers we found around the vic's nose and mouth could be a match to the white terrycloth towels used at the gym, but then again they could have come from any white cotton towel." Caine rubbed a hand through his hair. "We don't even have enough to get a warrant for his house. We can hold him for a while, book him for assaulting Officer Channing, but his lawyer will have him out on bail soon. For someone who works at a low-paying customer-service job, he sure does have a high-powered lawyer."

"Damn." Foregoing a chair, Jace sat on the table. "Do you get something from this guy? Something no one else can see or smell?"

"Tala thinks he's the victim's drug dealer. She's checking in with some buddies at narcotics."

"Tala thinks?" Caine lifted a brow. "Did she say what gave her that idea?"

Jace looked down at the floor. He knew what he was about to say was going to sound strange to Caine. But for some reason he couldn't pinpoint, Jace trusted her instincts. "She said she smelled it on him."

"Now that's odd. A human that can scent like a dog. What am I missing here, Jace?"

"Nothing. She's different, is all. I believe it when she says it."

Caine smiled then. Jace cursed under his breath. The last thing he needed was ridicule from a vampire.

"Different? Really?"

Jace jumped off the table and starting pacing the room again. "Look, just save it, okay. I'm wired and I need to run or I need to mate. One of those two things better happen soon or I'm going to explode."

Still smiling, Caine put up his hand, as if to ward off an attack. "I'll see what I can do about that run. But you have to do it quickly and quietly. Don't let anyone know I let you out."

"Sounds like I'm your pet," Jace growled.

Caine arched a brow. It was his way of saying everything he needed to say without saying a word.

"We don't need any more publicity on this case than there already is." Caine leaned back in his chair. "I can't even go out without being swarmed by the media."

"It's your vamp allure. Your pretty-boy looks were made for TV." Jace chuckled.

"Yes, and thank goodness I have a reflection or there'd be some freaked-out San Antonians right about now."

The conference door opened again and Tala burst through, excitement lighting her face. She moved straight toward Jace, completely unaware that Caine sat in the corner.

"We got him," she said as she handed Jace a piece of paper. "I knew I knew him from somewhere. He wasn't arrested, but he was picked up last year for suspicion of dealing Ecstasy—blue pandas, to be exact—at a local rave."

"Good digging," Jace remarked.

She smiled at him and it was the first honest look he'd seen from her. It brightened her face and her eyes. Jace found he couldn't tear his gaze away from her. In that one moment, she was enchanting.

Breaking the spell, he cleared his throat and asked, "How's your side?"

She twisted back and forth. "I'm okay. At first I thought that kick broke something, but it's just a surface wound. Nothing major."

Jace nodded, wanting to offer her more, but acutely aware of Caine watching them. He knew the vampire was looking for something to hold over his head. And his mooning over Tala would be just that certain something Caine would use.

"Great work, Officer Channing," Caine finally spoke from behind her.

Tala flinched and swiveled around. "Oh, I didn't realize anyone else was in here."

"You couldn't smell me?"

She glanced at Jace. He could see the embarrassment on her face. He had a sudden urge to hug her and soothe away the hurt.

"No. How could I?"

Caine threw up his hands. "Well, there goes my theory that you're really a lycan in disguise."

If he hadn't been looking so close, Jace would never have seen the shift in her eyes as Caine spoke. He swore he saw them glow for one second. A green so bright he couldn't even describe it. It had nearly taken his breath away. But then it was gone and Tala was turning away from him and walking toward the door.

"I just thought you'd want to know. I have a few hours off, so I'll be out of the lab for a while." She glanced at Caine then looked back at Jace. She was wringing her hands, Jace noticed. Nerves were surging through her like wildfire.

"I'll see you later." Without another word, she left the room, shutting the door behind her.

Standing, Caine moved toward Jace. He took the piece of paper Tala had given him and tucked it into his file folder. "I'll give this to Hector. I'm hoping it'll be enough to get a warrant for the guy's house." He patted Jace on the shoulder. "Don't look so surprised."

"What?"

"I never thought it would ever happen to me, either. Now, look at me." He held up his left hand and wiggled his ring finger. "I'm married to a woman I worship. A human woman with more guts and strength than any Otherworlder I know."

Shaking his head, Jace moved away from Caine and sat back onto the table. "I'm not sure what you're talking about, Chief. But I'm happy for you."

Caine continued to stare. Jace knew the vampire was trying to figure him out. Trying to sense his feelings.

Over the years, Jace had learned to control them around Caine. He hated being an open book to anyone. Even to the man who was the closest thing he had to a best friend.

After a few more minutes, Caine smiled and grabbed the handle on the door. "I'll see what I can do about that run."

Jace kept Caine's gaze. "Hurry. I don't know how long I can hold it in."

After Caine left Jace glanced down at his hands. He had them fisted tight. Unfurling his fingers, he saw the indentations his growing nails made in his palms. He was barely holding on. He wished Tala would come back. Being around her calmed him.

Just like a lycan mate would.

Running his hands over his face and into his hair, Jace shook his head. He was in deep trouble if he was thinking of her in that way. Nothing good could come of it. Lycans and humans did not mix. Not well, anyway. Like vinegar and baking soda. Explosive and messy.

He would shift, go for a run and expend all the pent-up adrenaline and frustration he had stored inside. Then he would come back with a fresh and empty mind, completely devoid of all unprofessional thoughts about Officer Tala Channing. At least, that's what he was hoping for.

Chapter 11

An hour later, Jace was running through tall green grass and around rangy fir trees, the moon cascading her enchanting light over his lithe wolf form.

The moon was his demanding mistress. When she called, he came. He had to. It was as simple as that.

The intoxicating smell of the night sent a shudder through his body. Damp grass and dirt brought a fresh tang to the medley of scents he discerned around him. It had rained a day earlier, finally bringing an end to the stifling heat of the Texas summer.

Jace loved autumn, especially when he got a chance to shift into wolf form and go running. And because it was nearing a full moon, the urge to do so fluttered through him constantly. Like an itch that would not stop even when scratched. Only changing forms and expending that pent-up energy by racing over the hills and through the grass brought relief to that kind of agony. That and mating.

But he knew, even in wolf form, he wasn't getting any of that anytime soon.

Once again, thoughts of Tala raced through his mind. The images were so vivid he swore he could smell her even now.

He took a tentative step out of the thick clump of trees and into the clearing, lifting his nose to scent the air. The spicy odor of female rolled into his flaring nostrils.

Tala.

She was here in the park, close by.

The snap of a twig had him slinking back into the shadows of the trees. He scanned the area, waiting for the source of the sound to reveal itself.

When Tala stepped into the clearing, Jace's whole body quivered with excitement. A powerful desire he didn't realize he harbored for her filled him. As a man, his head interfered with most of his emotions, but as an animal, it was pure—straight from the gut.

Enthralled, he watched as she took a few steps into the clearing, with her head lifted to the sky and the moon. Beams of pale light played over her face and he could see how she moved just slightly back and forth as if absorbing the night luminance. It was something he did every time the moon was out.

Why was she here? Of all the places in San Antonio, why did she come here to a park? It was certainly close to the lab. Well, the closest to the lab anyway. Still a twenty minute drive. Maybe she lived nearby.

Whatever the reason, Jace couldn't deny his attraction to her. Not here, not now. The way she looked in the moonlight was irresistible. He quivered with the need to go to her.

With her head still tilted up, Tala unbuttoned her jacket. She separated the two halves and looked as if she was offering herself up to the moon.

Unable to resist any longer, Jace took a step forward. A twig snapped under the weight of his paw and Tala turned toward him.

She met his gaze dead on. He knew she spotted him among the trees by the way her shoulders hunched and her knees bent as if to flee. From the way she reacted and the subtle change in her smell, he knew she recognized him as no simple wild wolf.

Need and hunger surged through him. Fear scented the air. Along with that he smelled excitement. His and hers, mixing together into a delicious medley. He took another hesitant step into the clearing. He could barely contain himself.

Just don't run. Just don't run.

Turning on her heel, Tala ran back into the trees she'd just come out of.

Without thought and only a feral need to chase, Jace ran after her. The hunt was on.

She was fast, but not nearly as quick as he was. It had been foolish of her to think she could outrun him. Wolves were great sprinters and amazing hunters. If she had read up on lycan behavior, she'd know that lycans hunted for two reasons: to eat and to mate.

She had to know he wasn't chasing her for a late-night snack.

As she bounded through the trees a few steps ahead of him, her scent tickled his nose. Fear, excitement, adrenaline. Three of his favorite things. Fear and adrenaline were expected. It was the smell of excitement that piqued his curiosity. She was obviously not as indifferent to him as he had first thought. But why now, while he was a wolf, did her excitement rage through?

He kept his gait easy instead of overtaking her. He wanted the game to continue. It was more enjoyable when it lasted longer. Anticipation upped his desire that much more. When he finally did take her down, it would be worth every extra minute of the prolonged chase.

But when he saw her climb the embankment to the road, a small economy car waiting there, he knew he didn't have any more time to play.

He put on the brakes and stopped just at the beginning of the rise. Pacing back and forth in the tall grass, he watched his quarry escape.

The car beeped indicating the locks disengaging just as Tala neared the front door and gripped the handle. Fumbling with the door, she finally managed to yank it open and jump into the vehicle. She hit her head on the roof and he saw her close the door on her foot. She opened the door again, yanked her foot in and slammed the door shut again.

He winced, knowing she was going to feel that later when her adrenaline stopped racing through her system.

As she started the car, she stared out the passenger window at him. A look of confusion furrowed her brow and narrowed her eyes. He imagined she was trying to figure out why in hell he had chased her and why she had liked it so much.

Because there was no mistaking the scent of female musk in the air. He inhaled it, reveling in the way it made his body tighten. But he'd get no release. Not now, probably not ever.

Her smell, her essence was now ingrained in his mind and in his body. There'd be no relief from it until he mated with her. But as things were between them, with the situation between their races and the case at hand, Jace knew that would never happen.

No matter how much he wanted it.

As she sped away in her car, he turned around and padded back into the trees to return to his pile of clothing and the vehicle waiting for him on the other side of the park. He'd come out here to burn off his frustration and need, but found as he trotted across the clearing, basking in the moonlight, that he trembled with even more.

Tala drove home as fast as she could, even blowing through the stop sign at the four-way intersection near her house. Once she parked haphazardly in the drive-way, she tore open the vehicle door and raced into her house. Slamming the door behind her, she locked it, engaging the deadbolt.

Only then did she relax a little and lean against the door, taking in deep measured breaths.

Even her slow breathing couldn't stop her body from quivering all over. Her teeth chattered from the intensity of her shivers. Adrenaline surged through her like quicksilver. She'd never been this pumped up before. Not chasing criminals, not running, not ever.

Why had she run? She knew he would chase her. His animal hunger would not have been able to help itself from pursuing her like prey. Had she wanted him to? To put her surrender in his hands, giving him the final choice?

Still shuddering from the rush of adrenaline, Tala pushed away from the door and wandered into her bedroom. She stripped off her clothes, went into the bathroom and turned on the shower. Hot water rushed out of the nozzle and hit her dead on. Closing her eyes, she let the gush of scalding liquid pour over her head and down her face.

Maybe she could scar the hunger from her mind and her body.

She hadn't fully realized how much she burned for Jace until she spotted him in his enthralling wolf form among the trees. The moment she had seen the animal crouched in the foliage, she knew it was Jace and not a wolf she needed to fear. It was the way he had looked at her, cautious yet curious, that had tipped her off.

He was breathtakingly beautiful. The silky luster of his dark brown coat gleamed in the moonlight. His eyes glowed like night stars. She had wanted to run her hands over his fur to feel the hard muscles underneath.

Biting down on her lip, she tried to push the thoughts from her mind. It was sick to think of it. He was an animal and she was a human. So what if the man inside the beast made her heart thump and her stomach clench with desire. He was not the same as her; they were worlds, species, apart.

Shutting off the water, Tala stepped out of the shower, grabbed a towel from the rack and wrapped it around her body. Still she shook. She decided to attribute it to the difference in temperature from the hot shower to the cool room.

But when pain ripped up her legs, forcing her to her knees, Tala knew it was more than that. Her body was reacting to Jace more than she had thought possible.

Grabbing hold of the counter, she pulled herself to her feet and yanked open the medicine cabinet. She scrambled through the other bottles and lotions searching for her plastic bottle. She found it in the corner, twisted off the cap and held it up over her head. Opening her eyes wide, she dripped the liquid into them. One drop, then two. Three. Four. She kept dripping until the shaking in her fingers forced the bottle from her hand and it dropped into the sink.

Clamping her eyes shut against the agony, Tala collapsed to the tile and curled into a ball. Her eyes felt as if they were melting. Maybe they were. Maybe she had used too much this time. With the urge to suppress herself, she may have wounded her eyes beyond repair.

A scorching pain razed over her as if burning her to the ground. She wanted to throw up from the agony of it, but she knew it wouldn't be that easy to find relief. Her penance was to suffer. And suffer she would for the rest of her days.

Because she knew there was only one way she'd ever find release. But to do so would be to damn her for an eternity.

Tala shook and quaked until finally sweet mercy found her and she fell asleep.

She dreamed of running. Of the moon. And of a wolf.

Chapter 12

The thundering of a heartbeat pulsed in her ears. She could hear the rush of blood streaming through her veins. The smell of grass, dirt and male wafted to her nose. She inhaled deeply, reveling in the delicious bouquet of scent. Shaking her head, shivers radiated from the end of her nose to the tip of her tail....

Tala was in the park again. This time *she* was the wolf.

And she wasn't alone.

Jace was there, in his ethereal beast form, standing in the clearing of the park, waiting for her to come out of the trees. Waiting for her to come to him.

Her whole body ached for him. She wanted nothing more than to bound into the grass and give herself to him. But she hesitated. Fear kept her still. She was afraid. Because with the desire came the realization of her true self. An identity she'd been fighting with her whole life. An identity that she feared and loathed with every breath.

She opened her mouth to speak, to tell him that she couldn't be his. That their union was not possible. That she was afraid of him and herself. But all that came out was a gruff bark and a series of low mewls.

Jace's ears perked up and he shook his muzzle and snuffled a few times. Remarkably, she understood him.

Don't be afraid. I won't hurt you.

Tears wanted to form in her eyes. Could wolves cry? She didn't know and she didn't care. He was so beautiful outside and in. He didn't deserve to be saddled with her issues. They were hers to deal with and hers alone.

Tala opened her mouth again and with it came a low keening. The sad sound of despair vibrated around her, making her shiver. Would he understand her? Understand that although she wanted to be with him, ached for him, she couldn't—not without sacrificing her entire world.

Without waiting for his reply, she turned and ran deeper into the woods.

She should have known he would chase her.

He was as stubborn as a wolf as he was as a man.

She could smell him as she bounded through the trees. His scent called to her, but she refused to listen. Refused to give in to it.

She ran harder, faster. Zigzagged around trees and

fallen timber. But she could still sense him behind her, matching her stride for stride, movement for movement.

She ducked under a downed oak, thinking she could lose him, but when she came up, he was on her. They tumbled over the brush and sticks in a tangled heap. Finally, Tala ended up on her side with Jace looming over her, his jaw open and teeth flashing.

Bending down, he took her by the scruff of the neck. His teeth bit into her fur and skin, but she felt no pain. Instead, her body woke. As if for the first time in her life. It thrummed and quaked for his touch.

A growl erupted from him. The sound was gruff and menacing but Tala heard the message, understood his meaning.

I can help you through this. Trust me.

Jace shot awake, his arms and legs flailing wildly. He nearly rolled off the cot he had been sleeping on. His heart thundered in his ears. Rubbing a shaky hand over his face, he looked toward the open door.

Lyra stood in the door frame, her brow furrowed. "Get up. We have a big problem."

Before Jace could respond, Lyra was gone. Shaking his head, Jace swung his legs off the cot, stood, twisted his body side to side and wandered out of the small sleep room and into the hall. It didn't take long to realize where Lyra and everyone else had disappeared to.

Jace followed the stream of people into the staff room. A crowd had gathered there in front of the TV.

Caine, Eve and Lyra stood at the back and off to the side with Hector. He looked around for Tala, but didn't see her in the crowd.

He pushed past a couple of lab techs to stand beside Lyra. "What's up?"

No one answered. No one had to. Everyone was watching the TV. The female reporter on the news told Jace everything he needed to know.

"During my coverage of the Samantha Kipfer murder, I have uncovered a startling piece of news."

A picture of Caine flashed on the screen. It looked like it had been taken just outside the San Antonio Police Department's front doors.

"This man, Caine Valorian, one of the crime-scene investigators, from a lab this reporter has been unable to determine, has himself a mysterious, sordid past. A quite remarkable past, if you ask me."

Another picture flashed on the screen. This one was much older, in black and white. It showed Caine. Looking much like he did now, except with longer hair. Instead of an Armani suit and tie, he wore a long surcoat and britches, circa 1890.

The pictures of Caine now and then were settled side by side. The resemblance was unmistakable.

"Is this the same man?" the reporter continued. "If it is, then maybe the rumors are true. Maybe we are surrounded by strange beings with dark and dangerous powers. If we are, then are any of us safe?"

The reporter went on about the controversial rumors

from the eighties about movie star Liam Wolf transforming into his namesake on national TV and how the government has been keeping the knowledge of the existence of Otherworlders a secret.

Jace cursed. Much louder than he intended, by the shocked looks on some of the lab techs' faces.

"You can say that again," Caine said.

"How bad is it?"

Caine put his arm around Eve, but kept his gaze on Jace. "Let's find a private place to talk."

Two minutes later, they were all seated again in the conference room. Caine sat at the head of the table. Jace perched on the edge of the table, too agitated to confine his body in a chair. He could smell the anxiety wafting off of Caine. And it worried him something fierce.

"The scrutiny on me has made this case even more fragile. I don't know how that reporter found out about pieces of my life, but she has, and has decided to reveal them on the local television news."

"I'd love to kick her," Eve reached over the table and grabbed Caine's hand.

Smiling at her, he said, "I know you would, my darling. But we need you on this case even more now. Having your sweet self in jail wouldn't do us any good." He squeezed her hand. "Because of this, I think it would be best if I stepped away from the investigation."

Jace bolted off the table. "What? That's insane. We can't let them push us around."

"It's not about us and them, Jace. It's about solving

the case. That's the main objective here. My involvement is just going to confuse the issue now."

"So what do you suggest?" Hector asked.

"Someone else will have to take lead on this case. And I'll have to be hands-off." Caine stared right at Jace.

Jace glanced around at the others. Everyone was eyeing him with varying emotions. Hector didn't look pleased, neither did Eve. Lyra regarded him with a mixture of interest and pity. None of this made him feel any better.

"Jace, you're going to have to step up to this, my friend."

"Why me?"

"Because I know you can."

Pacing, Jace tried to take in slow, measured breaths. He wasn't ready for this. He wasn't a front man. He did his best work behind the scenes.

"Why not Eve? She's human. She'll work better with them," he offered, waving his hand around to indicate the collective others beyond the conference door.

Caine glanced over at his wife and lifted her hand, linked in his, to his lips. "Because she is not a level-three investigator."

Eve pulled her hand from Caine's mouth. "Just because I'm not a level three yet, doesn't mean I can't do the job."

Jace shook his head. Caine had to know that Eve wasn't going to settle for a simple answer like that. Neither was he.

Sighing, Caine leaned back in his chair. "I'm sorry if that upsets you, Eve, but the truth is, you don't have enough experience to lead this investigation. Jace has the experience and the tenacity to see this case through to the end, regardless of the outcome."

"It's because I'm human and a woman, isn't it?" she demanded.

He grabbed her hand again and set it on his chest. "No, it's because I love you and I will not see you get hurt again. I don't want you in the front of this, Eve. This killer is on a mission. We missed him in Necropolis and you nearly died. I won't let that happen again."

Jace heard the agony in Caine's voice. He knew what torture the vampire had been through during the last case.

Jace swirled around and pointed his finger. "I'll cooperate, but I won't work *under* any human."

"You'll work directly *with* Hector," Caine responded, still clutching Eve's hand.

Jace glanced at Hector. The man had proved to be trustworthy and seemed to be at ease with their otherness. Since he likely had no choice, Jace agreed.

"Okay. Where are you going to be?"

"Here in the lab for now. Unless something else comes up and the lynching mob bangs down the doors with torches and pitchforks to chase me out or bring me down." Caine slid his stack of files across the table to Jace. "All our evidence is logged in there, photos of the body, crime scene, everything you need."

Jace picked up the folders and leafed through them.

There was a lot of information packed between the manila cardboard. He didn't know where to start. He had no idea how to lead others. It had never mattered to him before.

"I trust your nose, Jace. You've never been wrong."

"I am not calling you Chief or Boss, just so you know," Lyra smirked as she stood and came around the table to stand next to him. She punched him on the shoulder. "But I've got your back, as usual."

Eve nodded. "I trust Caine's judgment. You're a good investigator, Jace. I'm with you on this."

Although he never sought Eve's approval, it felt surprisingly good to hear her say she had faith in him. Even if it was all based on her husband's initial confidence.

"I don't care who does what, as long as we catch this guy," Hector said just as his cell phone chimed. Fishing it from his pocket, he answered on the third ring. After a few head nods and a couple of grunted responses, he flipped it closed and looked at Jace. "No time like the present to see what you're made of. We have another DB."

Chapter 13

Rage. Unbridled seething rage. That's what Jace scented the moment he stepped into apartment 810 of the Sun Vista Towers.

There was no mistaking the tinny odor of blood and death as he, Lyra, Eve, Hector and Tala entered through the front door and were directed toward the bedroom in the far corner of the small but tasteful suite.

The two officers standing just outside the bedroom doors were green around the gills and they averted their gazes as Jace led the team toward the crime scene. How bad the scene was going to be was written all over their faces.

"Hey, Mannie." Hector nodded to the younger

officer. Officer Vargas was printed on his name badge. "What are we looking at?"

Mannie read off his notepad. "Rebecca Simmons, age twenty-four. No sign of forced entry. A neighbor reported the smell at about 11:00 p.m.," he informed them. "The coroner's already in."

Bracing himself for the worst, Jace snapped on his latex gloves and was about to step into the room when the other officer stopped him with a hand on his arm.

"I'd put on shoe covers if I were you. It's a mess."

Jace took the man at his word and pulled plastic shoe covers from his kit and slid them on over his shoes. Eve, Lyra and Hector did the same. When Tala reached out for a pair, he shook his head.

"You're not going in."

She glared at him for a moment then looked away, turning to go stand with the other officers near the front door.

He had thought she was going to argue. But something in his eyes must have told her not to bother, that his mind was made up.

On another day, he would've looked forward to arguing with her, but not now. Not with the scent of death and destruction swirling all around nearly making him ill. He didn't want her to witness it. He wanted to save her from future nightmares.

Outfitted properly, Jace stepped into the bedroom with his kit in hand. Eve, Lyra and Hector followed close behind.

Nothing could have prepared him for the carnage he witnessed.

There were red shoe prints from the door to the bed and back. Also several prints were scattered around the bed and to the window. There was a wooden chair near the window. Blood drops surrounded it.

Jace glanced over his shoulder at Eve. "Find out how many people were in and out of here. Looks like three sets of prints."

She nodded, then exited the room.

"We need pics of the entire room and of these prints," Jace ordered.

Hector stepped to Jace's side. "I'll get the room shots." He lifted his camera and started taking multiple photos of the room, from the door, from the far side near the closet and from the window, giving them the entire overlay of the crime scene.

"I'll get the shoe prints," Lyra said as she pulled out the yellow plastic markers from her kit. "I don't think I'm ready to look at the body quite yet."

Jace didn't think anyone was ready to inspect the body. But it had to be done sooner rather than later.

Keeping left of the bloody prints in the beige carpet, Jace walked to the bed where their latest murder victim still lay on crimson-soaked sheets. The smell of blood and other bodily fluids nearly smothered him. But it was the sulfur that had his eyes filling with tears.

The stench was strongest right beside the body.

The coroner had just finished taking the liver temperature. He glanced up as Jace neared. "I'd say she's been dead around twenty hours." He scribbled his notes on his clipboard, then packed up his kit. "I don't think I've ever seen anything like this. Have you?"

Jace shook his head, unable to form any words as he surveyed the damage.

Kit in hand, the coroner left without another word, exiting the room the same way Jace had come in.

"Two officers came in the room. They said they walked to the bed to check her vitals and then back out again," Eve said from the doorway. "They didn't touch anything or move anywhere else in the room."

"Then this other set of prints has got to be our guy. And it's not a shoe print, but a footprint," Lyra offered as she set a marker beside a footprint by the window. She took several shots. "This guy must be huge. His print is a size sixteen."

Jace absorbed the information without comment. All he could concentrate on was the tragic condition of the body. Someone had torn the poor girl apart inch by inch.

Her body, from toe to head, was one huge roadmap of red lines. Cuts. Some were deep, some were shallow. There was no definite pattern, none that he could discern anyway. Maybe Lyra would see something different.

Just like last time, the magical symbols were there. Except instead of painted on with blood, they had been etched into the girl's flesh. Had to have been done with a small knife. A scalpel, perhaps, or maybe even a razor blade. Looking closer though, he noticed the cuts were irregular and jagged. Something a claw could make.

Shivering from the thought, he made a mental note to check the victim's bathroom for a razor. Maybe the perp used hers.

He winced, imagining the pure agony the girl must have suffered. He prayed that she had been unconscious for some it, unaware of what was being done to her.

"Lyra, I need you."

When she shuffled in beside him, he heard her quick intake of breath. "Oh, sweet Lord. He's escalated."

"Yeah, I kind of got that impression." Jace glanced at her. "Is the signature the same?"

Lyra lifted her hands and let them hover over the victim's torso then clamped her eyes shut. Within seconds, she opened her eyes and lowered her hands. She shook her head but kept her eyes on the body. "No. Nothing."

"It's not the same magic?"

She looked at him and he saw the confusion in her eyes. "Some of the symbols are the same but there's no magic."

Jace looked back down at the mutilated body. "Are you sure?"

"Yes. There was no ceremony here. Some of the symbols are missing and some are changed. I think on purpose."

From behind Jace, Hector offered, "Maybe it's not our guy."

Jace took in everything about the victim. Young, female, magical symbols on her body. Then he glanced around at the surroundings. They were in an apartment, upscale and trendy, in a busy complex. Not somewhere far from people. Not in an abandoned house or a scummy hotel room or a slaughterhouse. There were several melted black candles scattered around the room in no certain pattern. Not in a circle like the last time.

There were several differences here, but it was the similarities that made him certain this was the same murderer. That and the scent of sulfur. It was too strong, too distinctive to be a coincidence.

"It's our guy." Jace glanced back at the rest of the team. "I think we've just pissed him off." He turned back to the body.

"I'll search the hall and check with neighbors for anything out of the ordinary," Eve said.

Jace lifted his hand to indicate that he heard her but continued to regard the body on the bed. Maybe if he stared at her hard enough something would lead him to the killer.

Before, the murders were controlled and exacting. Purposeful. This savageness was without restraint. The killer had done this for a different reason. As a show to them? A message? If it was a message, Jace was taking it very personally.

"Do you think she's been sexually assaulted?" Lyra asked.

Jace nodded. "By the looks of this rage, I don't think he could've helped himself."

"Maybe we'll get some DNA."

"Yeah," Jace said as he picked up the victim's hand examining her nails. "Looks like she got a piece of him here, too."

"Here." Lyra handed him a nail scraper and a small paper evidence envelope.

As Jace scraped the dirt and what he thought to be skin from under the victim's nails, he shook his head. "I don't think DNA is going to help us much. This guy's not human."

"We can send it to Gwen. If he's in our database, we'll find him."

When Jace was done, he sealed the envelope and handed it back to Lyra. "Yeah, but I don't think he'll be in our database. I don't think he's one of us, either."

"Then what?"

"I don't know." Glancing around the room, Jace tried to take everything in, searching for that one thing that would give them the break they needed. As it was, they had nothing to go on, except a possible drug connection.

Jace swiveled around and looked at Hector, who was searching through the victim's dresser drawers. "We need to find out if they knew each other, have the same friends, frequent the same places. And I'd start with Hard Bodies."

Turning, Hector smiled. "I was thinking the same thing." He lifted his hand. In between his fingers he held a sports tank top. "Hard Bodies is just four blocks from here. I bet you she works out there."

"Looks like we need to have another chat with Darryl Rockland."

Hector stuffed the tank top back into the drawer and shut it. "I'll see what kind of background, habits and employment I can find out from the victim's next of kin."

"We'll go back with the body," Jace said, glancing at Lyra, then Hector. "Do you think we can have an audience at Mr. Rockland's interrogation?"

"I'll see what I can do." With that, Hector slid the evidence he collected into his kit and left the room. Jace and Lyra followed him out.

Tala was there waiting for them, pacing back and forth, wearing a path in the rug.

"It's drug related, isn't it?" she asked.

"It might be. Why?"

Nervously, Tala glanced at Lyra then back at Jace. He understood her message.

"Lyra, why don't you search the bathroom. Our perp may have gotten a razor blade from the victim's things to use on her."

Lyra smirked and shook her head, but said nothing. She moved down the hall toward the bathroom.

"Okay, spill it," he said to Tala.

"Did you find any Ecstasy?"

"Not that I was looking for that, but no." He eyed her. She looked nervous, jumpy. Itching to do something or get at something. "What makes you think there's any here?"

"If she knew Rockland, she'd be using for sure. I mean, the guy isn't exactly boyfriend material."

"We don't know that she even knew him."

Tala's eyes kept flicking toward the open doorway of the bedroom.

"I'm not letting you in there, so forget it," he said as he took a step sideways blocking her line of sight.

"Why?"

"Because you don't need to see that, Tala."

"I've been on the force long enough to have seen a lot, Jericho. Don't treat like I'm some fragile little princess."

"I'm not."

"I took down our only viable suspect, remember?"

Shaking his head, Jace sighed. "Fine. But don't blame me if you can't sleep for the next few days."

Nodding, she moved toward the room. He stopped her and handed her a pair of plastic shoe covers. "Here, so you don't track blood all over the place."

She visibly paled as she put the covers on. Then, squaring her shoulders, she stepped into the room.

Jace followed her, curious about what she was looking for. And how she would know where to find it. She had keen senses like an Otherworlder. Maybe she was psychic like Gwen, the lab technician. He wondered if she'd be willing to be tested after all of this. Maybe she could come to Necropolis to visit.

And maybe he needed his head examined thinking the way he was. Next thing, he'd be imagining what she'd look like snuggled into the king-size bed in his apartment.

Once inside the room, Tala made a beeline straight for the bed, her head down inspecting the carpet as she walked. When she reached the body, she glanced up and gasped.

Jace was there beside her in an instant. He put his hand on her shoulder. "Don't look at her. Keep at what you were doing."

Before he could warn her about the smell, she took in a deep breath and nearly gagged. She doubled over and started to hyperventilate.

He patted her on the back. "Breathe through your mouth."

Suddenly, she dropped to her knees. Jace panicked and made a grab for her to help her to her feet. Except she slapped away his hand, hard.

"Leave me alone. I found something." She stood and turned. In between her forefinger and thumb she held half a small blue pill with a panda stamped on it.

She had found their connection.

Chapter 14

"What do you mean the suspect's been cut loose?" Jace growled at Hector as they marched down the hall toward the lab together.

"His high-powered lawyer got him sprung."

"How is that possible? He was charged with assaulting a police officer."

They stopped at the doorway to the DNA lab.

"The D.A. dropped the charges after he agreed to drop the charges pending on you for police brutality."

Jace smirked. "That's ridiculous. I'm not even a cop. Did someone explain that to his lawyer?"

Hector scratched his chin. "I think, under the circumstances, the D.A. thought the less we talked about you, the better."

Frustrated, Jace ran both hands through his hair. It didn't help. Strands fell back into his face. "Yeah. Okay. Did you tell Caine? How did he take it?"

Smiling, Hector shrugged. "About the same way you did. Except his speech was a little more eloquent than yours."

Jace returned his grin. The captain wasn't turning out to be such a bad guy to work with. "Well, we still have the warrant, right?"

"Yes, that we do."

"Good. I want in on that." Jace lifted up the paper bag he was holding. "I'm just dropping the rape kit to DNA, then meeting with the others in the conference room."

"I'll see you in there." Hector tipped his head, then left.

Jace walked into the DNA lab with his evidence. The lab tech, Rick, jolted from his work when Jace approached him. The guy reeked of fear. Jace was getting tired of smelling that on almost every single person he ran into.

Setting the bag down on the counter, Jace grunted, "This is a rape kit. Please send it to the lab in Necropolis." He scribbled down the address on the transfer form.

Rick set down the microscope slide he was holding and leaned forward on his stool. "I can test it."

Jace scowled at him. "Nothing that is in there is human, buddy. You're not equipped to analyze this."

"I could try. I could learn."

Jace shook his head. "Look, this isn't school time. Learn on your own time, not mine." He turned and headed for the door. He didn't want to be late for their next meeting.

"It'd be a lot faster if I did the analysis and then I could email the findings to the lab tech in Necropolis."

Jace paused with one foot out of the room. He swiveled around and glared at Rick. He had a puppy-dog face with enormous brown eyes. There was something in them that Jace liked, that he trusted. Maybe he could give the kid a chance.

"Okay. But you call Gwen right now before you start. Let her know what you are doing." Jace returned to the counter and scribbled Gwen's number. He set the pen down with a click and stared at Rick. "And you make sure you call me as soon as you get any results."

"I will."

"I mean it. The second that printer beeps with a printout. If you don't…" He frowned. "I can't be held responsible for what I will do to you. Do you understand me?"

Rick nodded, his eyes wide. He looked like a boy being scolded by his father.

Before Jace could crack a smile, he left the lab and made his way down to the conference room.

The door to the meeting room was open. He walked in to find Caine, Eve, Lyra, Tala and Hector all there seated and waiting for him. It felt strange having them wait for him. Usually he was just one of them, sitting, waiting for the chief to debrief them.

Now, it was the other way around. Surprisingly, the sensation wasn't all that unpleasant.

As he marched to the table, he had to stop himself from sitting in a chair along the side. Instead he walked to the head and stayed standing.

"The autopsy went as planned. Nothing abnormal showed up. Nothing prohibited. She was indeed raped, violently, and we did collect a DNA sample. As we all can guess, it won't show up as human. Your lab tech, Rick," Jace nodded at Hector, "and Gwen in Necropolis are going to work together on this." Caine's eyebrows went up at this news. "I thought it would do this lab a world of good if they brushed up on their Otherworld anatomy since, according to the media, we are about to invade and overrun humanity."

The corners of Caine's mouth twitched, but he remained silent.

"Until we get the results, the only thing we have to go on right now is the drug connection between the victims." Jace's gaze found Tala's. That zing he had come to expect between them cracked across the air, hitting him in the gut. He had to suppress the urge to reach across the table and touch her. "Thanks goes to Officer Channing for her findings."

Blushing, she lowered her gaze to the table.

Hector cleared his throat. "Unfortunately, our guy's been cut loose, but we have a warrant for his house and to bring him back in for questioning."

"The partial shoe print came back as a certain type of hiking boot. I looked it up and it is usually worn by mountain climbers. So that matches our rope, which is also of rock-climbing quality."

"What I wouldn't give for a fingerprint right about now," Hector said, the exasperation in his voice evident. His shoulders sagged.

"At this point, I don't think it would help us much."

"Why?" Caine asked. "I can see those gears grinding, Jace. You have a theory."

After running a hand over his face, Jace slumped into the chair behind him. "I don't think we're dealing with human or Otherworld. It's something else. The sulfur smell was strong at the last crime scene, too. I've never encountered something like that before."

An odd look flashed in Caine's eyes. Jace caught it right before the vampire turned toward Eve and grabbed her hand on the table. Jace thought it looked like fear.

"That night in the slaughterhouse, do you remember anything more about what happened?" Caine smoothed his thumb over the back of her hand. Jace knew he did this to comfort her. Eve had gone through hell when she had been kidnapped from Caine's home.

"When I found you, you asked me if we got both of them. Do you still think that there was another person there besides Mel Howard?"

Eve kept Caine's gaze, but Jace could see her throat working. He was positive she was trying to suppress the anxiety she was feeling just thinking about that night she was kidnapped.

"I had a sense of being around more than one person.

I couldn't see anything. It was a cold, creeping feeling of constantly being watched."

Jace understood that feeling well. When he had been in the freak show, he had experienced that icy sensation regularly.

"And Mel kept referring to *he. He* wouldn't let me do this, *he* wouldn't let me do that. At one point I thought someone else was pulling his strings, but later, in the hospital, I assumed I'd imagined it and that Mel was a nut job with a split personality."

When she was done speaking, Caine pulled her to him and wrapped an arm around her shoulders, pressing his lips to the top of her head. Relaxing, she snuggled into him.

Jace envied their obvious comfort and love for each other. He wanted that someday. A lover and a friend. He avoided glancing at Tala as he thought of that someday.

He coughed into his hand and continued with the briefing. "Well, I think it's obvious now that there was someone else in Necropolis participating in the murders and in the ceremonies. Now this someone is in San Antonio running loose and is pissed at us for following him here."

"Demons."

Jace, as well as everyone else, swiveled toward Lyra. She was staring down at her open folder, the pen in her hand forming figure eights on a blank sheet of paper.

"Lyra, let's not go there again," Jace said.

She looked up at him and he could tell immediately that she was angry, but there was something else. Tropidation maybe? He usually trusted her insights because she was usually correct. Smugly so. But he couldn't fly with her demon theory. It was just too damn impossible.

This, from a werewolf. He could hear her words echoing in his mind.

"Would you clarify that, Lyra?" Caine inquired.

"Well, we thought the markings were all about someone doing a demon summoning. Believing in the possibility of calling the dark forces forth. A moron dabbling in the dark arts. What if the dark forces are already out and about? And he's just calling home for some reinforcements."

Silence cocooned the room.

Jace glanced at every team member. Each had their own expression of contemplation on their face. Hector looked like he was going to pass out. Jace imagined the man was dealing with a lot of information. Here he was sitting around a table with creatures from his nightmares, discussing the existence of the demons of hell.

Jace shook his head. "No. Sorry, but I don't buy it. It's not possible."

"Jace, how can you say that sitting here in this room with a vampire and a witch at your side? At one time, we were considered impossible."

"Yeah, but our existence is purely scientific, not mystical. We're products of strange and rare genetic codes." He waved his hand to indicate the others in the room. "For demons to be real…"

"Evil would have to exist?" Lyra finished for him.

He nodded. "Something like that."

"You're the one that said this guy wasn't human or Otherworld."

"I know, but what I meant was that he's something new, something different. A race we've never encountered before. Maybe the sulfur is a byproduct of some sort of chemical imbalance in his system...not the remnants of brimstone from the pits of hell."

Caine raised his hand. "Okay, we could probably argue this all morning, but it's not getting us anywhere. It's nothing short of normal for the two of you to disagree, but at this point in the case it's irrelevant. We don't have enough evidence to support either theory. Right now the best thing to do is to move forward. Let's execute the warrant, search Rockland's home and find the evidence we need to link him to the murders or at least to the drugs found with the victims."

Pushing away from the table, Jace stood. "Okay, let's roll then."

Everyone else stood, as well.

"I won't be going with you," Hector announced. "I have another matter I have to deal with. I'll make sure there are a couple uniforms available to take with you."

Jace nodded. "I appreciate it."

As they marched out single file, Caine grabbed Jace's arm and pulled him back. When they were alone, he dropped his hand.

"A word of warning, my friend. Don't be too sure about your feelings. If the evidence is pointing in a certain direction, don't let your reasoning stop you from seeing the damn arrow."

"I know, Caine." Jace scoffed. "But demons? Come on. It's illogical."

"The definition of logic is 'the principles and criteria of inference and demonstration.' But it also means 'to force a decision away from or in direct opposition to reason.'"

He patted Jace on the back and left. Damn vampire! Always has to have the last word. And in this case, the last word had sent shivers racing down his spine.

Chapter 15

Darryl Rockland lived in a one-bedroom apartment in a nice neighborhood close to the fitness center he worked at and the second victim's apartment complex.

At five o'clock in the morning, the team and two uniformed police officers lined up in the hall in front of Darryl's door. The landlady was nervously shifting from one foot to the other, her keys jiggling in her shaking hands.

The young officer from the last crime scene, Officer Mannie Vargas, knocked on the door. "Darryl Rockland, this is the San Antonio Police Department. We have a warrant to search your apartment."

Several seconds ticked by with no response from inside the apartment.

Mannie knocked again. "Open up. It's the police."

Still no answer.

The officer nodded to the landlady. "Open the door, please."

She shuffled, still in her housecoat and slippers, to the door and opened it. Mannie motioned for her to step away from the door. She did so quickly.

Grabbing the door handle, Mannie slid out his weapon and slowly opened the door. "Police. We have a warrant."

He went in, followed by the other officer. The team waited in the hallway for the word to enter.

After a few minutes, Mannie peered through the open doorway. "It's all clear."

"Okay, everyone take a room," Jace instructed. "We're looking for anything to link this guy to our victims."

Eve and Lyra went into the apartment. Tala was about to, when her cell phone shrilled.

She glanced briefly at Jace then flipped her phone open. "Channing."

Jace watched her as she spoke into the phone. The more he was with her, the more appealing he found her. The way her lips moved, the way her auburn hair glinted in the sunlight and the way the little lines at the corners of her eyes creased when she was thinking. And especially the way she smiled. Because it was rare to see one on her usually stern face.

But as she closed her phone and slid it back into her pocket, she was smiling. "We caught a break."

"Tell me."

"I found out where the blue pandas have been coming from. There's a known rave location not far from here." She glanced at her watch. "If we go now, we'd just be hitting them as they close up shop."

Jace grinned, sharing her excitement for the chase. "All right." He moved into the apartment. "Hey, we've caught a lead to a known rave near here. We're going to go check it out."

Mannie lifted his hand. "I'll go with you."

Jace nodded to him, then glanced at Eve and Lyra. "You ladies are on your own. The other officer can take you back to the lab."

"Cool," Lyra said. "Just the way we like it, right Eve? There's too much testosterone when you're around, Jace."

Eve just smiled. "Hey, I like testosterone. I'm married to a vampire, remember?"

Lyra shook her head but returned Eve's smile.

Chuckling, Jace left the apartment to chase his new lead. Well, technically it was Tala's lead. He just wouldn't tell her that he considered it his.

When he, Tala and Mannie arrived at the old art gallery, there were streams of young people wandering out of the building. Some looked normal and tired from dancing into the wee hours of the morning, but others weaved back and forth on the road looking like they were going to fall down at any moment.

And none of them seemed to be bothered by the police cruiser that Mannie had parked on the sidewalk.

Jace got out of the car and he, Tala and Mannie entered through the main doors into the big building that was once a busy art gallery.

Music continued to thump from the multitude of speakers situated around the open floor space. Some hardcore partiers were still dancing. Some even on top of the speakers.

The sound was deafening to Jace. His teeth were rattling from the vibrations. He touched Mannie's shoulder and pointed to the corner, where the DJ was still spinning his records. Mannie nodded and made his way across the floor.

Jace followed him, motioning with his head for Tala to follow behind.

As the three of them walked across the dance floor, some of the revelers finally took notice of Mannie's uniform and made a beeline toward the nearest exit. By the time they reached the DJ booth, most of the remaining partiers were making their way to the doors.

When they approached the booth, the overweight white DJ had just finished shoving something into his pocket. Likely drugs. Fortunately for him, they weren't looking to bust him.

Mannie nodded to him and showed him the picture of their suspect, Darryl Rockland. "Do you know this guy?" He had to lean into the guy's ear to speak.

Jace heard every word from where he was standing a couple of feet away.

The DJ shook his head, his blond dreadlocks nearly

smacking him in the face. "No, man. Never seen the dude."

"Are you sure?" Mannie insisted, flashing the picture again.

"Hey, man, I'm not doing anything but having some fun. There's nothing going on here but a good time."

Yeah right, Jace thought. He glanced around the room, looking for anything that would lead them further. From around a stack of floor speakers, Darryl Rockland bounced into view. The guy was laughing and chatting with a group of teenage boys. Jace watched as their suspect handed a small plastic bag to one of the boys, and the boy gave him a wad of money.

And Bingo was his name-o.

Tala must've seen him at the same time, because she tensed beside him. He glanced at her and saw her neck muscles quiver and her jaw twitch. She looked like an animal ready to pounce on her prey. *Interesting.*

Jace smacked Mannie on the arm and nodded toward their suspect.

The cop nodded and the three of them moved from the DJ booth and toward Darryl. Fortunately, he hadn't noticed as they advanced on him. He was too involved with the trafficking of Ecstasy to minors.

But one of the teenage boys did notice them and he nudged Darryl with his elbow, then turned to make his own escape.

Jace cursed under his breath as their suspect made them. Tensing up, he prepared for a chase. Within seconds, Darryl was running across the dance floor toward the back of the building.

Without any hesitation, Jace was in hot pursuit. As he ran, he sensed Tala and Mannie behind him. Tala was a lot closer than he would've guessed. She was fast.

Because of his head start and vicinity to the back of the building, Darryl pushed through the back exit door a few seconds ahead of Jace. It afforded him enough time to be rounding the corner of the alley having already tossed something into a neighboring yard just as Jace managed to burst through the metal door. There was a heap of wooden crates off to the side stacked against the green chain-link fence and if not for his quick feet, he would've careened right into them.

The door smashed open again and Tala came rushing through. She was not as lucky or as quick. The tower of crates toppled over as she barreled into them and the fence shoulder first.

Skidding to a stop at the mouth of the alley, Jace considered racing back to help her. He was making his way back when he saw Tala's head pop up from the broken wood and her hand waving in the air.

Mannie burst out of the back door and immediately aided Tala to her feet.

"Go Jace! Don't let him get away!" she called.

The spot of blood on her forehead made his pulse pound. He hated the sight of it marking her perfect skin. His blood boiled just imagining any amount of pain she endured.

Good lord, he'd never felt this much concern for anyone before. Oh, sure, he certainly didn't want anything to happen to Caine, Lyra, even Eve, or anyone else at the OCU, but he'd never hesitated when something needed to be done by the mere thought of them hurting. This was a new thing for him.

The worry coursing through him for Tala was nearly staggering.

"Is she all right, Mannie?"

The cop nodded. "She's fine, just a couple of cuts."

"Oh, for cripe's sake, Jace, you're losing our suspect!" she yelled.

He could discern the frustration in her voice and he knew she was fine. That's all he needed to hear.

"Okay, but I think he tossed something into the next lot. Check it out."

Without any more hesitation, Jace turned back around and raced out of the alley to track Darryl. Little did their suspect know that this was exactly what Jace was born to do. In seconds, Jace had Darryl's scent.

It was hunting time.

Chapter 16

Tala breathed a sigh of relief when she finally saw Jace disappear around the corner of the alley. For a second, she thought he was going let their only suspect get away just because she had done something careless and embarrassing.

The fact that his concern warmed her in all the right places was inconsequential.

Brushing off the dirt and splinters of wood from her pants, she let Mannie inspect the cuts on her head and arm. She wanted to tell him that they were nothing, that she felt little to no pain and they would likely be gone in a couple of days. She'd always been a quick healer.

Too quick for some people. She could hear her

mother's voice. *Always keep the bandage on longer. You don't want people asking questions.*

Tala swatted Mannie's hand away when he started probing her other arm. "I'm fine."

He held up his hands and backed away. "Just trying to help."

"I know, but I don't need it."

"I'm going to go radio dispatch and let them know our suspect is on the run and investigator Jericho is in pursuit." Mannie grabbed the handle to the back door. "You'll be okay to search for the dump, won't you? I don't think there are any more little crates to jump out at you over there." His smirk told her he was making fun at her expense.

"Ha, ha. Make yourself useful and grab Jace's evidence kit when you come back."

"What makes you think I'm coming back?" he scoffed.

She gestured to him with her finger. A gesture that told him exactly what he could do with that comment.

Laughing, Mannie disappeared back into the brick building.

Now that he was gone, Tala could concentrate on tracking down the item that their suspect had dumped. She was good at finding things. And there was no one around that would inquire on how she did it. She could get down on all fours and sniff out the trail if she wanted. She wouldn't, of course. She had a little more dignity then that.

Glancing at the fence separating the alley from the barren lot next door, Tala couldn't find an immediate opening. She'd have to jump it if she wanted to start her search. Or she could walk down the alley to the street and go around. But what if she missed something? What if Darryl tossed more than one thing? She opted for jumping the fence.

Once over, she immediately started searching the ground. Sweeping from right to left as she walked, Tala eyed every little piece of trash and debris that was scattered all over the barren concrete lot. She toed over every rock and empty soda can she came across.

After walking halfway across the lot, Tala finally noticed the gathering shadows cast by the morning light around her. She had been so intent on searching for evidence of drugs that she didn't notice she wasn't alone any longer.

Raising her head, she saw several youths standing around her. By the looks of the four males and one female, Tala didn't think they had come over to help her out. Lifting her nose, she smelled the sickly scent of fear and realized it was her own.

"What are you doing here, sugar?" The biggest male asked, the gold on his wrist glinting in the sun.

Tala eyed the group and noticed gang colors. She wasn't familiar with which one they belonged to, but by the way they were all standing and eyeing each other, they were looking for trouble. Even though she was armed, a young female cop alone was a perfect mark to make a name and rank in gangland.

"I'm doing my job. So I suggest if you don't want

any trouble, you best be moving away and allow me to do it." Glancing quickly over her shoulder, she noticed that one of the male youths had stepped in behind her out of her peripheral vision. Putting her hand on the butt of her gun, she took a step to the side trying to outmaneuver them.

She didn't want to draw her weapon. In the few years she'd been a cop, she'd hadn't had to. She knew cops that went their whole careers without pulling a gun. She wanted to be one of them. She didn't want to be in a situation where she'd need to, especially against a bunch of kids.

"What's the matter, Miss Piggy, feeling a little scared?"

Fear *was* needling its way through her system. But that wasn't what was worrying her. Fear was natural, especially in a situation like this. It was the growing excitement and anticipation of something more coursing its way over her body that concerned her. It didn't seem like a normal response.

Unsnapping the strap on her holster, Tala wrapped her hand around the butt of her weapon. "I will not ask you again to step away from the scene and go about your business."

That started a round of snickers through the group. The leader swiped at his nose and smirked. "Woman, this *is* our business."

Tala drew her weapon and pointed it at the leader. "I will give you two minutes to comply with my request or I will arrest all of you for obstruction of justice."

Another round of snickers rippled through the group.

The leader took a step toward her. She could see he was high on something. His face was passive, cold, unfeeling. His eyes were wide, the pupils dilated. He had to be pumped up on PCP or worse to make him act like he had a death wish. No sane person would keep antagonizing an armed police officer.

"Oh, that's a big gun, pig. But I bet you want something even bigger to play with." He grabbed his groin with his hand and wriggled his tongue at her.

The punk was starting to make her angry. And the scent of his arrogance and youth was tickling the sensitive endings in her nose. Thoughts of how much fun it would be to chase him across the parking lot filled her mind. Images of him down on the ground cowering beneath her as she tore at his flesh with her teeth made her shiver. Saliva actually pooled in her mouth.

Her hands started to shake. The gun wavered up and down. "Please," she pleaded. "Please go away. You have no idea what you're dealing with here."

"Hey, Tommy, I think she's going to cry," the youth to her immediate right said to the leader.

Tommy took another step toward her. The barrel of her gun only a foot away from his chest. "Are you going to cry, little piggy?"

There was a ringing in Tala's ears. The punk's voice sounded much too loud in her head. Wincing, she tried to shake the sound from her mind. Her head felt like it was going to split open from the pressure.

Damn it! Something was wrong with her. There was a hunger inside her that she'd never experienced before. It ripped at her insides like claws shredding paper. A need to chase, a need to hunt. She wanted nothing more than to bring Tommy down like an animal.

"Oh, God, please don't," she pleaded.

Tommy laughed. "Get on your knees bitch and maybe I'll let you go."

"Let's just do it, Tommy, and get out of here," the only girl said.

He glanced around at the others then nodded.

Lifting their arms, the group of youths threw rocks at Tala. Big chunky rocks flew through the air and pelted her in the head, arms and legs. One right after another came hurtling toward her. They must've picked them and piled them into their pockets before they had even advanced on her.

Instinctively she raised her arms to protect her head. But one sneaky apricot-sized stone smacked her in the cheek. Pain rippled through her and she knew she'd been cut. She could feel the trickle of blood over her skin.

Something burst inside her. Something large and hungry tore free.

"You'd better run," she growled, with a voice so low she hardly recognized it as her own.

Faster than she could ever imagine, Tala holstered her weapon and struck out at Tommy, the leader. The bottom of her foot connected with the top of his kneecap. She held back a little because she didn't want to snap his bone. Although she had been tempted. And the temptation tasted like ambrosia on her tongue.

Howling in pain, he dropped to the ground. She stood over him and sneered. "I told you to run."

Someone hit her in the back of the head. Pain ripped through her. She collapsed to a knee, her vision swimming in and out. Blood dribbled down her forehead and into her eyes.

Wiping at her face, Tala's vision faded then came back, but everything was stained red as if she was looking through a crimson lens. Was it from the blood or something else peering out from her eyes?

Chapter 17

Livid that he had lost their only suspect, Jace ran back around the corner and into the alley behind the old art building where he had started. He couldn't believe he lost the guy's trail. Darryl Rockland was one lucky son of a bitch.

If Jace hadn't used those precious moments to make sure Tala hadn't hurt herself when she tumbled into those wooden crates, he would've caught the suspect.

Damn his fool heart.

As he moved down the lane, a strong scent of blood wafted to his nose. Lifting his head, he took a deep breath. It was close.

A sudden growl of rage echoed across the lot triggering his hair to stand on end and his hackles to rise.

Tala.

Turning his head, Jace caught sight of something that tore the air from his lungs.

In seconds, Jace cleared the fence and raced toward the grisly scene. She was there, but not as he had left her.

He had known there was something different about her. Her smell had been too strong, too enticing. He had reacted to her on a very basic level. An animal level. Now he knew. Deep down inside, she had hidden her secret self. Her true self. Her lycan self.

But by the state she was in, it was obvious that she had never shifted before.

The agony swimming in her eyes as he approached nearly sent him reeling. He could just imagine the pain she was enduring. The pain subsided once a lycan fully shifted either way, but to be stuck in between must've been nearly unbearable.

She was crouched low next to a young man's body, her hands pressing him to the ground and her glowing green eyes shifting back and forth nervously. The boy was sobbing, but seemed unhurt. So far, anyway. A few bruises here and there. By the look on Tala's face, she was certainly considering harming him.

Blood leaked from various wounds on Tala's face, arms and torso. Her clothes were crimson and her hands streaked red. The blood smelled like her own. She had been attacked and was acting out. She was in a rage. All young lycans suffered through it when it was their first time.

Thankfully, he saw that her lips were unstained. She had not tasted the blood. At least, he hoped she hadn't. It proved more difficult to come back to human form once a lycan had a taste for the kill.

He neared her, his hands out to his sides in a submissive manner. "Tala, I can help you."

She growled low in her throat and hunched her shoulders.

"Let me touch you. I can help you force it back."

She shifted her weight to her back feet, preparing to leap forward. The long talons poking through the tattered remains of her boots clicked on the cement as she moved.

Jace stopped moving and kept her gaze. Before, he had talked down one of the young pups in his pack during his first night from breaking a vampire's neck. He could do this. It was no different.

Except he hadn't been falling in love with that young pup.

"This is your fault." She winced as she spoke through elongated teeth and protruding jaw. "I was doing okay before you came."

Jace could just imagine the agony tearing over her. "I want to help, Tala. Please let me."

"You can't." She grunted then leaped forward over the youth's shivering body. She hit the ground on all fours and started running.

He couldn't let her go. Not like this, not in the state she was in. He feared she would hurt more people and herself. He couldn't live with that. Swiveling around, he leaped and made a grab for her.

He managed to snag her around the waist and they both came crashing down to the hard cement. Tala ended up underneath him. The moment she landed on her back, she started to struggle and fight her way out of his hold.

Jace tried to keep her still, but her new talons were sharp and vicious. After a few well-placed swipes at his neck and chest, he had to let go. Any more injuries like that and he'd bleed to death no matter how fast he healed.

Slick with his blood, Tala slid out of his arms, turned and ran. He let her go for now. He'd track her after he called for an ambulance for the teenager bleeding on the ground. He wondered what he had done to force the beast from Tala. Because he knew she was too wound up, had too tight a grip on her animal, for it to come out for no reason. She had had it so locked up that he hadn't been able to smell it in her.

Taking out his cell phone, Jace called 911. "I need an ambulance at 222 Dawson Street. There's been an animal attack. Please hurry."

He slid the phone into his pants pocket then quickly crouched down next to the young man. He grabbed Jace's arm and started to babble. "Oh, thank God, you showed up, man. She…that bitch was going to kill me."

"Nah, she wouldn't have killed you, man. Just ripped your guts open." Jace smoothed a hand over the guy's head. "I wonder what you were doing here, though."

"Nothing. We weren't doing nothing, I swear."

"We?" Jace glanced around the lot.

"We just wanted to see what she was doing. This is our lot and we were just protecting our turf."

Nodding, Jace understood now. He took in the guy's clothes and the expensive jewelry he was wearing. Gang paraphernalia. "Yeah, I'll bet you were." Running his hand along the boy's neck, Jace found the pressure point he needed and pressed down. "Listen to me. You and your friends were attacked by an animal." The boy's eyes starting rolling in his head. He was close to losing consciousness, just the way Jace wanted him to. "You don't know what it was. But that's what happened." Another second ticked by and the boy was out cold.

Standing, Jace wondered if he should take the SUV to track Tala or do it the old-fashioned way, on foot. Four feet, anyway. He was a better tracker as a lycan. Besides, he didn't know the city streets, so finding Tala through the network of roadways with a vehicle would be next to impossible.

After another quick glance around the area, Jace unbuttoned his pants and let them slide to the ground. He kicked out of them, took off his socks, his shoes and tore off the remaining remnants of his bloody shirt. He shoved the shoes, socks and bloody shirt into his pant leg, then tied up one end. The other end he looped around his neck and fastened it on. When he shifted, at least he'd have his clothes and phone with him still.

Glancing around once more to make sure there were

no curious eyes watching him, Jace went down on all fours and forced the shift through his body. Pain tore through him as bones and muscles grew and shifted positions. A scream tore from his throat as hair, talons and teeth pushed through his flesh like iron nails hammered through a wooden board.

When he was done, sweat slicked his entire body, but he shook it off as if just coming from a bath. Once the pain receded enough to concentrate, Jace raised his muzzle and scented the air. Within seconds he had Tala's trail. After a final quiver from toe to tail, he took off across the parking lot in pursuit of his quarry.

He was starting to believe this woman might be his one true mate.

Jace tried to stay to the shadows and alleyways as he tracked Tala through the city. It was full daylight now and the citizens of San Antonio were wide awake. In some instances she made that impossible when she barreled across busy streets, seemingly unaware as vehicles came to screeching halts to avoid hitting her. He tried to find alternate, less conspicuous, routes to take around the busy streets, but sometimes there was just no other way.

He could just imagine the news reports flashing on TV later today. *Large wolves spotted in the city. Keep your children indoors.*

It also didn't help that the teenager would be found with claw marks on his body. Jace had sympathy for the poor animals in the area that would be put down due to this incident.

After a half hour of running across the city, Tala seemed to slow. Her scent came to him on the warm Texas breeze. It was full of anguish and confusion. But also of familiarity.

She was heading home.

It would have been instinctive for her to flee to some-place safe and secure. He just hoped her neighbors weren't home as the half-wolf half-human woman bounded up the steps to her door. In this state, Tala wouldn't be able to keep her secret for much longer.

He stayed back and watched as she crept along the quiet street of a clean older neighborhood. Hiding behind an azalea bush, Jace watched as she moved across the road and collapsed onto the lawn of a small bungalow. He could see the heaving of her chest and the spasms in her hind legs. She was trying to shift back.

Crouching onto his belly, Jace closed his eyes and willed the change to come. Within minutes he was back in human form, his slick naked body shaking violently. Taking the wreath of clothes from around his neck, he slid into his pants, socks and shoes, shoved his ruined shirt into his pants pocket and ran across the street to aid Tala.

When he got there, she was convulsing. Crouching next to her, he put his hand on her forehead and one on her stomach to hold her down. Closing his eyes, he sent waves of healing power into his hands. He hoped it would be enough.

If she couldn't shift back, she'd remain in half form forever. And her mind would be lost. He'd seen it before.

in his pack. The young woman had ended up committing suicide.

He wouldn't let that happen to Tala. Not when he had just found her and connected to her.

Finally the heat of his power coursing through the palms of his hands quieted her spasms. Breathing heavily, she blinked up at him, agony bringing tears to her eyes. She was still half-formed.

"You need to force the shift back, Tala. It's the only way."

She shook her head, tears streaking down her temples to drip onto the grass. "I can't." Her voice was muffled by her overgrown fangs.

"You can. You're a strong woman. Dig deep inside, you'll find the power to do it."

Shutting her eyes, Tala tensed all the muscles in her body. He could feel them bunch and quiver under his hands.

"That's it, Tala. You're doing it."

Mesmerized and awed, he watched as her feet shrank, the talons on her toes disappearing into themselves. The coarse auburn hair on the back of her hands receded into her pores. She was almost there. She just had her face to shift back. It always proved to be the hardest part. It was the place where the shift started.

Grunting in pain, Tala started to quiver again. Her teeth had started to shrink, but then something had stopped it. Her eyes sprang open and he could see the panic and terror in them.

She grabbed his arms and sobbed. "It hurts too much. I can't do it. I feel sick."

"It's all right. Just let it happen. You're almost there." Jace set both his hands on her cheeks. "Feel the heat from my hands. Concentrate on that."

He was no healer like Lyra with her spells, charms and incantations. But lycans had the power to mend their own. If connected on a spiritual level, lycans had the possibility to heal many wounds.

He sensed a beginning of that type of bond with Tala.

Calming again, Tala shut her eyes, but she didn't relinquish her hold on his arms. If linking them together aided her shift, he would gladly touch her wherever she wanted.

After a few more tense minutes, her jaw finally receded and her teeth slid back. With one last gasp, Tala tensed and pushed everything back to normal. She opened her eyes, smiled at him, then promptly passed out from the exertion.

Wiping the sweaty strands of hair from her brow, Jace pressed his lips to the tip of her nose. "You did good, little wolf."

He slid his arm under her shoulders and under her knees and picked her up. Walking up the three steps to her front door, he kicked it open and carried her through.

He'd fix the door later, but right now, Tala needed to sleep. And he needed to think. Everything had changed. Tala was not the human woman he'd thought she was. She was Other, like him. Now he had no wall keeping back his feelings. And that was the thing that scared him the most.

Chapter 18

*B*lood. *The smell of it nearly made Tala gag. It was everywhere. All around her. Splashed on every inch of her naked flesh.*

She lifted her crimson-stained hands up to her face and started to lick them clean.

Tala bolted up from her sleep. Panic suffocated her and she clawed at her mattress. Her bedsheets were tangled around her arms and legs and she felt smothered. Ripping the cotton away from her body, she finally collapsed back on the bed naked and sweating.

She glanced around her room, confused and disoriented. How did she get home? Hadn't she been at a crime scene?

Then it came crashing down on her like a two-ton weight.

The vacant lot. The teenagers. And the blood.

"Oh, God," she wailed. Her stomach roiled in utter revulsion. Groping her way to the side of the bed, she scrambled off and rushed into her bathroom. She grabbed the bottle of mouthwash on the counter and poured some in her mouth. After swishing, she spat it into the sink. Slamming open the medicine cabinet, she rooted around for her drops. They weren't there.

Panic surged over her and she dropped to the floor and scoured the drawers and cupboard under the sink. Still nothing. Where did she last put them?

"Looking for this?"

Swirling around, Tala saw Jace standing in the doorway, her plastic bottle of eye drops captured between his fingers.

She reached for him. "Give it to me."

He danced out of her way. "How long have you been using this?"

Unconcerned that she was still naked, she stood and rushed him, trying to pry the bottle from his fingers. He was too strong, and she was much too weak. Dejected, Tala pushed away and rushed into her living room. Maybe she had drops in her purse.

"How long, Tala?"

She ignored him as she searched for her purse. She found it underneath her coffee table. Unzipping it, she dumped the contents onto the table and searched through it.

"I took the one from there, too."

Closing her eyes and clamping down on her urge to scream, Tala sank back into the fluffy pillows of her sofa. She let her purse fall from her lap. "You have no right."

Shivering, she finally realized that she was naked. She wrapped her arms around her chest, suddenly very aware that she was exposed and Jace had seen her.

Jace came around the sofa, handed her a robe and sat on the edge of her coffee table near her. "It's silver nitrate, isn't it?"

She glared at him, but took the offered robe and wrapped it around her body. "You have no idea what I have suffered."

She saw the twitch at his jaw and thought he would protest, but he remained quiet and watchful, allowing her to make her case. She didn't like the way he looked at her, his eyes full of disappointment and scorn. That was exactly the same look her mother had given her the day Tala discovered her...condition. Mutation, her mother had called it.

"You look at me like we're the same. Like we're kindred spirits." She bit out the words between clenched teeth. "But we're not. I had the chance to be human. Do you understand that? My mother is human. And because of her rape I was conceived."

"She was raped by a lycan?" he asked, his voice quiet, careful.

Tala nodded, tears now streaming down her face. "She never told me the entire truth. She just said that my father left her when he found out she was pregnant. Not until the night…the night I turned thirteen and started to change. Then she told me the awful truth." Swallowing down the urge to sob, Tala continued, "It was then that I learned what a freak I was. And my mother told me of a way to keep that side of me controlled."

"A freak?" Jace exploded off the table in a fury. She winced at the unrestrained violence of it.

He began to pace in front of her. "You are not a freak, Tala. Oh, my God, woman, do you have any idea how beautiful and special and unique you are?"

He thought her beautiful? Even after seeing her half-formed and grotesque?

"I'm sorry for what happened to your mother, Tala. I'm sure it was horrific and terrible, but that doesn't make you those things. You can't condemn yourself for something that happened to your mother."

Tala shook her head. "Can you imagine what it was like for her when I was born? To look at me and know that I carried his genetic material, too? That possibly one day I might grow fur, fangs, howl at the moon?"

"That still doesn't give her the right to make you believe that you're a freak. You should have been nurtured and supported because of your differences and not been forced to poison yourself in shame of them."

She pushed to her feet and rounded on Jace. "She did the best she could for me."

"I'm sorry, but it wasn't good enough."

Anger rippled through her. Anger and sorrow and guilt. Thoughts she didn't even realize she harbored popped to the surface in a fury of emotion. Raising her hand, she slapped Jace across the face.

"How dare you? You know nothing about me or my situation. You have no idea what my mother suffered or what I've suffered." She pushed him. "Get out! Get out of my house and get out of my life! You have no business being here!" She went to push him again, but this time he caught her wrist, keeping the flat of her palm pressed against his chest. She could feel his heart racing.

It felt so much like her own.

She didn't want to feel a connection to him. But she did. It hummed between them like an electrical current.

"I was raised in a circus. In a freak show," he said, his voice deep and icy cold. "When I was nine, my parents, in wolf form, were killed by hunters and I was left to fend for myself."

"Jace, I…"

He shook his head stopping her next words. "Let me finish." He took a deep breath and continued, "I started my shift early so after they died I remained in wolf form most of the time. I even found a real wolf family that tolerated me enough that I didn't go hungry. But they, too, were killed and I was captured. And when my secret was revealed I was sold to a circus."

Fresh tears sprang to her eyes. She could feel Jace's

agony pounding her as he told his story. In his eyes she saw the cold, hard truth of his tragic life. He had suffered more than she could ever imagine.

"I'm so sorry."

Tala tried to pull away from his touch. She didn't want to know any more. Feel any more. His pain was too much. Somehow during the recounting of his tragic tale, they had become linked. Irrevocably bound. The connection thumped and beat like a pulse. As if it was alive and had a mind of its own.

She didn't want to feel any empathy. Because it forced her to face the truth of her own life. And the shame she had harbored for so long. That had always been her wall, her protection from others. She didn't want anyone to get to know her, to become too close.

But now Jace was smashing down those walls. And she didn't want to see the person standing behind the barrier. The person she truly was. Because those walls had also been protecting her from herself.

He held her wrist tightly with one hand and covered her hand with his. "I know what suffering is, Tala. I know what it feels like to be ashamed of who you are. But after seven years of torment and despair, I found my way out of servitude and I survived. You can, too."

Did she want a way out? Did she want to finally embrace that part of her that she struggled so hard to keep locked up? Was she ready for what came with it? The ridicule, the prejudice and the fear.

And ultimately her mother's disappointment.

Shaking her head, she said, "I don't want to be lycan. I don't want to be different."

"But you are, Tala. You are so much more than human. Can't you understand that?" Letting her hand go, he cupped her cheek with his hand and stared deep into her eyes. "Are lycans really all that repulsive? Do I repulse you?"

She wanted to say yes to prove her point. But she couldn't utter the words. Jace was the exact opposite of repulsive to her. He was beautiful and sensual and she wanted him on so many levels it was impossible to understand them all.

She shook her head, not able to lie to him while he stood so close to her. The heat of his body enveloped her, soothing her from head to toe.

"Then why would you think that you are?" He rubbed a thumb over her bottom lip. "You are more radiant to me than any human."

The connection between them spiked as if an energy flow had rushed through the wires. She nearly gasped from the intensity of it. Liquid heat pooled between her legs.

Panicked by the pure explosiveness of the sensations coursing through her body, Tala retreated backward, pulling away from his touch. But he wasn't going to make it easy on her. Surely, she had expected nothing less from this stubborn man.

For every step she took back, he took a step forward. By the time she'd backed up into the wall, they had moved across her living room to the doorway of her bedroom. A very dangerous place to be, considering the desire flowing through her like a wildfire.

"Stop running, Tala. You don't have to be afraid of what you are."

"I could've killed those kids," she breathed, her voice so low it nearly stuck in her throat.

"But you didn't. You kept your head. However tenuous it seemed, you did control your beast." He raised his hand and touched her again, but this time it was a light brush on her neck and over her shoulder as if searching for a way into her soul. "With my help you'll keep control. You can learn how to shift back and forth. There are so many cool things about being a lycan. I can show you all of them."

"Like what?"

"You can use your heightened senses for crime-scene work. I know you already use your nose." He grinned and tapped her on the tip of her nose. "You can even use it to find out if someone is lying to you." He trailed his hand down her arm to her wrist and encircled it with his fingers. "A person's pulse spikes when telling a lie. Even if that person thinks they can control it, it's not enough to keep me from feeling it."

She tried to pull from his touch, but he held her there, staring into her eyes.

"Are you aroused, Tala?"

"No."

His eyes flashed. "Liar." He squeezed her wrist

tighter, drawing her to him. "Don't fight it, Tala. Together we can tame your beast."

A quiver of hope vibrated inside her heart at the pos-
sibilities. Could she just let go and discover what that
truly meant? With Jace? It seemed too good to be true.
Nothing was ever that simple.

She wanted to back away but she had nowhere to go.
What Jace offered was tempting, but it was not something she was sure she could do. Not now. Not after
living a lie for so long. Not when it was so much easier
to continue to live that lie than to open up her heart and
her soul, exposing herself completely.

"I can't, Jace. I won't let it loose. It's too late for me."

She saw the sadness in his eyes, but also the flare of
something primal. It frightened her. It also excited her.
Deep down inside, the spark that bonded them flared,
eager to explore, eager to be set free. But would she
survive the release?

He took another step toward her, nearly pressing his
body into hers. She shuddered as his scent filled her. He
smelled of the earth and storm clouds and sex.

"Oh God," she whimpered. "You're too close. I
can't breathe."

Jace ran his palms down her arms and grabbed her
hands. Lifting them, he set them on his shoulders and
breached the short distance between them, pressing his
hard, hot flesh against her. "Let go, Tala. Don't be afraid
of it." Leaning down, he brushed his lips over her temple,
and whispered, "Let go, I'll catch you. I promise."

Glancing down at his chest, Tala touched the wounds she'd inflicted. They were healing faster than humanly possible, but they still looked raw and painful. How could she live with herself knowing she could inflict this type of injury?

"Do they hurt?"

He shrugged. "A little. But I don't mind. I'm hoping you'll give me a matching set on my back by the time we're done with each other." The corners of his mouth lifted.

The image of Jace riding her while she raked his back with her nails flashed through her mind. Tala groaned, unable to resist him any longer. She wrapped her hands around his neck and pulled him down to her lips. Warmth spread through her. She gasped from the sensations coursing through her. And finally let go.

Chapter 19

Jace thought he was prepared for the cascade of emotions that he knew would flow through him the moment he touched her. But nothing could prepare him for the overwhelming reality of it. It was like molten desire, liquid and scalding hot, racing over him, through him. Possessing him completely.

As her full, soft lips moved over his, her tongue tasted and teased. Jace filled his hands with her breasts. Her nipples hardened through the fabric of her robe as he caressed them with his fingers, enjoying the way she gasped each time he moved.

He gobbled up every sound she made, eager to hear more. He wondered if she'd moan his name as he took her. The thought left Jace achingly hard. Moan it, scream it. He didn't care, as long as it was him she called for.

Desperate to feel the warmth of her skin against his, Jace pulled on the cloth tie. The fabric barrier separated, exposing a sliver of bare skin to his hungry eyes.

With the sash undone, he moved his hands over her warm flesh. He groaned, then body slammed the impulse to take her right here.

Blind to everything but the sensations in his hands, Jace moved his fingers over her, exploring the soft dip of her waist. So fragile, yet so strong. Her ribs tickled his palms as he stroked his way up to her perfect breasts. This time when he cupped her, she gasped and pulled back from the kiss.

"Jace," she moaned. "It's too much. I can't think."

"Good," he growled as he looked down at her. "I don't want you to think. Just feel."

Her eyes fluttered closed as he massaged her nipples with his thumbs. He loved the lost look on her face. One of abandonment. Shifting backwards, he pulled her robe down her arms and off her body so he could look his fill of her lithe form.

"You're so damn beautiful."

Her eyes opened and he saw the pink stain her cheeks, and the beginning glow in the green of her eyes. She moved to conceal herself.

He covered her hands with his. "Don't hide. Not from me. Never from me."

Sighing, she let her arms fall to her sides. Jace looked her over from head to toe, drinking in her sublime body. She was so striking. Powerful with sculpted muscles and sleek lines. She had a body made for running and for sex. He couldn't resist any longer. His desire was ripping at him, clawing its way out. He needed to have her, possess her utterly.

Growling, he moved in, wrapped his arms around her and crushed his mouth to hers. The kiss left him dizzy. Jace trailed his hands down her back and molded the firm cheeks of her rear, then he picked her up. Instinctively, Tala opened her legs and wrapped them around him. Gripping her tightly, he nibbled on her bottom lip and made his way over her chin to her neck. Her skin tasted like syrup.

He nuzzled in between her legs, effectively pinning her against the wall with his body. With the liquid heat of her center pressed against his groin, Jace thought he'd died and gone to heaven. Surely, there wasn't a more divine place to be than nestled between Tala's thighs.

His whole body trembled with desire, a ferocious insatiable hunger. He needed to be inside her now. He would perish if he had to wait much longer.

"I want you so bad," he growled into her ear, after licking the side of her neck. "Do you want me?"

She nodded, her lips pressed together tightly. He could feel her body quivering under his touch. The smell of her desire enveloped him. It was an exotic spice in his nose. Lord, he'd never smelled anything as delectable in his life.

"Say you want me." He nipped at her chin.

"I do," she breathed. "I want you so much."

"Where?" Jace rocked his hips, grinding his shaft into her warmth. His arms quaked with strain and repressed need. He couldn't hold back for much longer. But he wanted to hear her words. Needed to know how much she desired him.

"Inside of me." She gasped, urgency tightening her grip. "Now, Jace. Please, now."

With one hand, he unbuttoned his pants and freed himself from the confinement of the fabric. Moving his hand up, he sought her. She was hot and wet and ready. Unable to wait any longer, he guided himself in between her legs. With one swift thrust, he buried his entire length inside.

In that instant he found his Shangri-la.

Tala had no idea that sex with Jace would feel so incredible…so wild and primal. Every nerve ending in her body came to life as he moved, slowly at first, then he picked up the pace before finding a delicious rhythm that sent shivers from her toes to her scalp.

She'd had lovers before, but she had never felt so alive with them. With Jace, it was as if the world had exploded with color, texture, taste and smell. She could discern everything around in a brilliant kaleidoscope of color.

The skin on the bottom of her feet tingled, as did the backs of her knees. Places she never knew could react with such hot intensity flared to life. Her whole body became one multifaceted erogenous zone.

But deep down, Tala could sense something else trying to surface. The feral part of her howled inside her head. Sensing Jace's lycan, it longed to be released. It wanted out to mate.

Panic squirmed through her. Squeezing her thighs against Jace's waist, she pushed at his shoulders. It was becoming too much. She couldn't handle the multitude of sensations bombarding her all at once.

Sensing her panic, Jace slowed his movements and looked her in the eyes. "Am I hurting you?"

She shook her head, too overcome with emotion to speak.

Bringing his hand to her face, he stroked her cheek and kissed her lightly on the lips. "It's okay. Just let go. You don't have to hold back with me." He kissed her again, this time nipping her bottom lip. "I can take whatever you give."

By God, she wanted to let loose. Her desire was bubbling up like molten lava, waiting to erupt. Tala had always been so afraid of letting it out with other men. Deep down, she was afraid of hurting them. She knew she possessed the strength to.

But with Jace, it would be different. He was more than human. He was more than any man before. He could handle everything she let out and then some. In fact, he was eager for it.

Digging her fingers into his shoulders, she returned

his kiss with eagerness, nibbling and teasing his tongue. A growl rumbled out of him as he buried a hand in her hair and countered, biting at her lips.

He rocked between her legs as they kissed. With each thrust, Tala thought she'd go mad with pleasure. It didn't just ripple over her skin but surged through every inch of her body like shore-crashing waves of pure unadulterated bliss.

Streaking her hands to his back, she searched for purchase, something to hang on to as he took her up, pushing her close to the edge of orgasm. Shifting his stance, he gripped her butt cheeks tight, pushed her hard against the wall and buried himself deep.

Gasping, she dug her nails into his flesh and raked them across his flesh.

Jace returned her fervor by clamping down on her shoulder with his teeth. Pain and pleasure washed over her and clashed together into a delicious torment. Moaning, she urged him on as she writhed against his body.

"More," he growled, licking the spot where he had just bitten her collarbone. "I want more."

Settling her in his arms, Jace carried her into her bedroom. She squeezed her thighs tight around his waist and held on, but that didn't stop her from feasting on his lips, groaning into his mouth with each stride of his powerful legs.

When he reached the bed, he dropped her onto the mattress, stood back and tore down his pants. He kicked out of them and gazed down at her with fire in his eyes.

His intense gaze made her stomach flip and her thighs tingle. No one had ever looked at her like that. As if he could feast on her from head to toe all night long. The wild primal things that she hungered for him to do were in his eyes.

She reached out for him, gripping him around the waist and pulling him to her. He was gorgeous. All rippling muscles and hard, rigid planes. Tala touched his stomach, trailing her fingers around his navel. She loved the way he flinched and his muscles quivered under her touch. She had power over him and she reveled in it.

Urging him closer, Tala pressed her lips to his sternum and licked her way down to his belly button and back up again. His skin was fevered, hot to the touch.

He moaned and wrapped his hands in her hair. Tilting her head, he stared down at her. The muscles in his jaw twitched with barely controlled passion and his eyes flashed like burnt amber. "By the moon, woman, you drive me wild."

She smiled at him and dug her fingers into his backside, taunting him to prove his statement.

Jace took the challenge and pulled her up to his hot, hungry mouth. He kissed her hard, devouring her lips with teeth and tongue.

She couldn't get enough of him. He tasted like the night bathed in pale moonlight, crisp and clean. Like a cool mountain spring, natural and pure. Tastes she'd been longing for her whole life.

Tala was burning up inside for him. If he didn't take

her now, she'd scream. As she nibbled on his bottom lip, she moaned into his mouth. "Enough foreplay."

He needed no more encouragement.

Breaking the kiss, Jace spun Tala around and pushed her forward onto the mattress. She put out her hands in time to break her fall. She tried to turn, but he was there, pressing up against her backside, his legs in between hers, forcing them apart. Jace's hands clamped down on her hips, preventing escape.

She was inflamed beyond reason as he nuzzled his erection into the juncture of her parted thighs. Digging her fingers into the mattress, Tala bit down on her lip as he slowly entered her, inch by delectable inch. He was so big, so hot and tantalizingly male. She thought she'd go mad before he fully seated himself.

Once sheathed inside her, Jace started to move. With every thrust forward Tala pushed back, meeting him, matching his rhythm. Pleasure swelled over her, into her and through her. She became a purely sensate being. Every inch of her body ignited and flared and flashed. Finally, she let go and gave Jace complete control. She was too enraptured to do anything but hang on.

She closed her eyes, riding the waves of pure pleasure that crested over her and twisted her under.

Groaning, Jace fell forward onto her back, wrapping his hands around her body, his hands around her breasts, as he buried himself deep. She could hardly breathe with the intensity of emotions cascading around her.

As Jace continued to slide in and out of her, he moved

one hand down and cupped her where they joined. She gasped when he slipped two fingers over her, circling the sensitive nerves at her center. As he pressed one, then two fingers on her, she could feel her orgasm building to a crescendo.

Tala could feel her legs tighten, her breath hitch in her throat. She cried out Jace's name as she spiraled down toward a liquid pool of pure pleasure. Release found her and pushed her in, drowning her in sensation without thought or care.

Everything around Tala exploded with color and sound and texture. She thought she'd go blind and deaf in the bombardment.

She crawled forward on the mattress in an attempt to escape the almost painful orgasm, but Jace held her down, coaxing more from her with his clever fingers and his tongue on the back of her neck. Quivering uncontrollably, she gritted her teeth as another wave of pleasure swept her away. Jace followed, emptying himself inside her with a violent shudder.

Chapter 20

Jace didn't want to move but knew he had to the second his cell phone trilled from his pants pocket. There was going to be hell to pay for them leaving the scene. Especially without the suspect or the drugs Darryl tossed. And Jace imagined the hysterical kid wasn't going to help matters any.

While Tala had been asleep earlier he had checked in at the lab. Caine had been none too pleased with the situation. Officer Vargas had come back to help Tala and found her gone. Instead there had been an ambulance attending to an injured teenager raving about a werewolf.

Jace told Caine the edited version of what happened, leaving Tala's transformation out of the picture. There was no way that he was going to be the one to out her, not even to Caine.

The vampire informed Jace he would take care of it. But hearing the icy calm of Caine's voice, Jace knew there would be consequences that he was going to have to deal with when he returned to the lab. He was sure he would be able to handle whatever Caine dished out. It certainly wasn't the first time he'd ended up on the vampire's bad side. And it definitely wouldn't be the last.

Scrambling off the bed, he grabbed his pants and dug out his phone. "Jericho." He turned and watched Tala as she rolled out of the bed and slid her robe back on.

"Mr. Jericho, it's Rick. From the lab."

"What's up?"

"You told me to call you as soon as I had any results. Well, I think you really need to see it to believe it."

Jace sighed. "Look, I've had a really tough day, can you just tell me what's going on?"

Tala padded past him and disappeared into the bathroom. He heard her turn on the tap. The sound of water trickled out from the room.

"The DNA from the kit? Well, it's not on my database."

"Which I already told you."

Rick chuckled nervously. "Yeah, but it isn't on the Otherworld one, either. Gwen is just as floored as I am."

"So what are you saying? That you can't identify the DNA?"

"Yes, that's exactly what I'm saying. Whoever or whatever this belongs to is a completely new species."

"I'll be there in twenty minutes." He flipped the phone closed, slid it back into his pants pocket and then put them on. He padded back to the bed and sat down on the edge, cradling his head in his hands.

Tala came out of the bathroom with a wet cloth in her hand. When she neared the bed, she crouched on the floor and began to scrub at the stain her vomit had made on the rug.

He watched her and knew she was upset. He could tell in the jerky way she moved and the scent she was giving off. Guilt. Remorse. And still that shame. But now he wondered what exactly she was ashamed of. What she was or that she had sex with him?

"We need to go back to the lab." Jace rubbed his hands over his face and through his hair. That was the most his hair was going to get combed today.

She nodded but didn't meet his gaze. After one final rub on the carpet, she stood and walked back to the bathroom.

"Tala."

Ignoring him, she continued and disappeared into the bathroom again.

"Stubborn woman," he grumbled under his breath.

"I heard that," she said from the bathroom.

Standing, he stalked over to the doorway. "Good. Because it's true." He paused just inside the door.

She stood at the sink, her hair up in a tight ponytail, her face freshly washed. And he wanted her all over again. Just as fiercely. Maybe more so. Now that her scent and her taste had been imprinted in his soul, he was lost to her.

She met his gaze in the mirror and tensed. He knew she could sense his growing desire. It was hard not to, when his pants were becoming constricted once more. He shifted his stance to accommodate his arousal.

The corners of her mouth lifted. "Is that all you think about?"

"Pretty much. Especially around my female. I can't help it. You smell so damn good."

She swiveled around and sneered. "I'm not your damn female, Jericho."

"The hell you aren't," he snapped back.

Whoa, where did that come from? His female? When had that happened?

She stomped across the tile of the bathroom and pushed past him to go into the bedroom. He stared at her retreating back and realized with blinding clarity that he had indeed branded her as his own. He could smell it on her. She belonged to him whether she liked it or not. By the way her eyes flashed at him when she turned around, he figured she was none to happy about it.

Well, neither was he. But there was nothing either one of them could do about it now. Branding was permanent. Lycans mated for life.

She stormed back across the room at him, the green of her eyes sparking like emerald fire and her robe fluttering behind her. "Look, just because you and I—"

"This wasn't just casual sex, Tala."

Coming to halt right in front of him, the next words died on her lips and she clamped them together then sighed. "It can't be anything more. And I want my eye drops back."

Gripping her by the arms, he pulled her to him and crushed his mouth to hers. No, nothing between them could ever be casual. It would always be hot and frantic. They were doomed to be forever urgent, impossibly frenzied.

Wrapping her arms around him, she kissed him back just as hard and just as fiercely. She tasted like sunshine. Hot and sultry. She was all flash and fire, his Tala. Just like him.

He broke the kiss and stared her in the eyes, willing her to feel the power zinging all around them. "Does that feel casual to you?"

"No," she said, her voice barely a whisper.

"I didn't think so. And I flushed the silver nitrate down your toilet."

"Great. So what are we going to do about all this?" she asked, her eyes flaring again. He could read the desire in them.

"Well, I'd love to take you back to bed." He nuzzled his face into her neck. Moving his hands down, he cupped her rear end.

Something stirred the air. Lifting his head, he turned toward the door of the bedroom.

An older petite woman stood in the door frame. A murderous look wrinkled her face. Tala's mother, he had no doubt. They had the same expressive green eyes.

"I knew something was going on," she said.

Tala pushed out of Jace's arms and pulled her robe tighter around her body. "Mother. What are you doing here?"

She held out her hand. "You gave me a key, remember?" The copper glinted in her palm.

"For emergencies only."

Jace could smell the woman's hatred floating across the room like the spray from a skunk as she looked him up and down. He wrinkled his nose as it hit him full force, almost making him stagger backward. The woman was definitely going to be a force to reckon with. Jace had no doubt she was right this moment thinking of a million ways to get her daughter away from him.

It was too bad he loved a good fight. He would not let what happened to her in the past be the reason that he and Tala couldn't be together.

Tala rushed across the carpet and herded her mother into the other room. "Whatever you have to say, can you save it for later? I have to get back to the station."

"It didn't look like you were going anywhere but into a bed."

"Mother, please. Could you just leave? And I'll call you later."

Jace could hear the desperation in Tala's voice. Her mother had a tight grip on her psyche. He imagined she doled out the guilt and shame with the same vigor some mothers did food. He feared that Tala had tasted so much that she'd never be able to purge herself of the woman's grip.

"He's one of *them,* isn't he?"

"Mother, please leave."

"I've been watching the news reports on that other one, Valorian. It's not right, Tala. I knew you were in trouble. I knew it. And I come here and find *him* nibbling on your neck."

Jace had had enough. He couldn't sit by and let Tala be treated like this.

He wandered to the bedroom and leaned against the doorjamb. Both women turned to look at him. He smiled. "Babe, do you have a T-shirt I could wear?"

Tala glared at him. He preferred that look to the one he'd seen earlier on her face. One of desperation and helplessness.

"Just who do you think you are being here with my daughter?"

"Jace Jericho, ma'am. I'm here because Tala and I are working together on a case and we're also sleeping together. In fact, right before you barged in we were talking about making our relationship permanent."

Claudia's mouth gaped but no sound came out. She opened and closed it several times like a guppy gasping for water.

"We were not!" Tala exclaimed as she marched toward Jace, her fists clenched tight. She punched him hard in the shoulder. "Quit making trouble. I'll get you that damn shirt then we are leaving."

Over the shock of what he had said, Tala's mother bunched her hands and set them on her hips, giving him a look that he was sure could wither the tallest oak tree. "I don't know what your game is but Tala is not to be trifled with. She's…different and fragile and doesn't need the likes of you messing with her head. You'll just confuse her."

"Lady, I think you've done a fine job of that all by yourself."

She stalked toward him. When he growled at her, she stopped midstride.

"Tala deserves to experience her true self without shame or guilt. So I suggest you back off and let her do that."

"How dare you?" Her voice shook. She was quickly learning that she couldn't push him around like she did Tala.

"I dare. And I'll dare even more if you keep pushing me."

Tala came stomping out of the bedroom. "Enough." She tossed Jace a shirt. "Put that on so we can go." She looked at her mother then pointed to the door. "You can see yourself out, Mother."

With an indignant sniff, her mother turned on her heel and marched across the living room and out the front door, slamming it smartly behind her. When she was gone, Tala stalked back into the bedroom. Jace followed her in, feeling quite smug.

"Well, not a perfect first meeting, but I'm sure she'll learn to love me over time."

She whirled on him, her eyes glowing. "Shut up,

Jericho. I don't want to hear another word." Grabbing some clothes, she tossed a T-shirt at Jace, stomped into the bathroom and slammed the door shut.

Chuckling, Jace slipped the T-shirt over his head and down his torso. Fantastic. Their first fight. He couldn't wait until the make-up session. It was just too bad they didn't have more time to do what he had in mind before they went back to the lab.

Chapter 21

Rick, the lab technician, was bouncing like a pogo stick when Jace and Tala marched through the door.

"Gwen's on speaker phone," he announced as he shoved a piece a paper into Jace's hand. "Here's the printout."

"Hi, Gwen."

"Hey," Gwen's deep voice came from the phone.

Jace looked over the DNA analysis. He was no expert, but even he could see the oddities present.

"There are XY and XX chromosomes." He looked at Rick.

The tech's eyes were dancing. "I know."

"Did I mix up the samples? Were the vic's fluids in the same kit?"

Rick shook his head. "Even if they were mixed up, the machine would be able to differentiate between separate DNA strands. No, these chromosomes are in the same strand for one individual."

"Male and female?"

Rick nodded enthusiastically.

"Gwen," Jace said.

"I found no vampire, lycan or witch chromosomes in the sample. I've never heard of anyone having both male and female DNA." She chuckled. "And don't get me started on everything else that's wrong with the code. It's like it has been pieced together from a whole range of different species, animal included."

Jace frowned. "So, what, are we looking for a six-foot-tall humanoidlike amphibian with size sixteen feet?"

"Beats me," Gwen said.

"You're supposed to be a genius, Gwen. Find me something reasonable to work with."

Even through the speaker, Jace could hear her angry intake of air. "Yeah, sure, Jericho. Whatever you want."

"We'll work on it together, Mr. Jericho," Rick assured him. "I'm sure we'll find an answer."

Jace nodded just as Lyra bounded into the room. "There you are. Man, I've been looking for you everywhere," she said. "Everyone's waiting in the conference room."

"Okay." He nodded at Rick again. "Call me if you come up with anything." Then he followed Tala to the door. Lyra was already in the hallway waiting for them.

Before he could leave, Rick rushed up to him and

whispered in his ear. "Hey, what's Gwen like? She sounds really hot. Do you think she'd like me?"

Jace looked Rick up and down, taking in his green Skechers, stained black jeans, wrinkled lab coat and greasy dull-brown hair. He smiled. "Go for it. Gwen likes it when a guy is aggressive. It turns her on." He slapped Rick on the back and walked out of the lab with a grin on his face.

As they walked down the hallway to the conference room, Lyra glanced back and forth between Tala and Jace. "Hey, what happened to you guys earlier? I heard you left the crime scene unexpectedly."

Jace sensed the immediate tension in Tala. It was subtle, not something an untrained observer would notice. But Lyra was very well-trained and she never missed a clue.

Lyra's eyes widened and she opened her mouth. But she thought better of what she was going to say when Jace growled at her. She flashed him a quick cheeky grin and walked into the conference room.

Caine, Eve and Hector were already seated around the table. Lyra slid into a chair beside Eve. Tala took a seat next to Hector.

Jace could feel Caine's gaze on him when he walked in and took up a position at the head of the table. He avoided looking at the vampire and only glanced at everyone else. Tension filled the room. Jace almost felt light-headed from the varying degree of smells coming off their bodies.

He pinched the bridge of his nose to stem the flow of air to his head. "Okay, where are we?"

Eve lifted her pen and began speaking. "Lyra and I found a pair of shoes in Darryl Rockland's bedroom closet. We matched the tread to the partial print you lifted from the house." She slid the photos of the perp's partial shoe print across the table to Jace. "We also found a pair of black leather gloves in the perp's house that had orange fibers on them. The fibers match the kind of rope that was used to hang Samantha Kipfer from the ceiling."

"Did you find any rope in his house?" Hector asked.

Eve shook her head.

"He could've gotten it from the fitness center where he works. I noticed that there was a climbing wall," Lyra added.

"Sure sounds like he's our guy," Hector said.

Caine jumped in. "But we don't have the murder weapon, and there's no DNA or fingerprints to link him to the scene." He shuffled through his crime-scene photos and pulled the one of the other murder. "Is there anything linking him to this one?"

Jace shook his head. "The footprints we found are a size sixteen." He glanced down at the photo of Darryl's shoe. "This guy's what, a size thirteen?"

Lyra nodded. "Yeah, that's what he measured." She pushed her chair back and leaned forward. "Plus, we didn't find anything with him that says witchcraft or demonology. I found nothing in his house that felt like magic. If he had any ability I would have sensed it."

"The only thing we have linking the two murders is the presence of drugs and the magical symbols," Jace said as he stared down at the mug shot of Darryl Rockland. They were missing something. Well, many somethings. "I think he's just a drug dealer." He looked up and met Tala's gaze. "What do you think?"

Tala shifted nervously in her seat and cleared her throat. "Darryl's a punk. He deals drugs. I don't think he's a murderer. Not to this degree. Out of self-defense, maybe, but not in cold blood. I don't think he has enough backbone for it."

Caine nodded. "I agree with your assessment, Tala. I think our suspect is involved but he's not in this alone." He looked around the table, meeting everyone's gaze. "But I think we already knew that some time ago."

"The DNA from the second scene is…not normal." Jace slumped into a chair and put his hands on the table, fiddling with the DNA report from the lab. "As I thought earlier, we are looking for some new being. The weird thing is it has both female and male chromosomes."

That sent a ripple of confusion across the table. Everyone shifted uncomfortably in their seats.

Lyra laughed, but not with humor. "Well, I think we can safely say that it's male. It did rape our second victim and ejaculate."

"Maybe we're dealing with a shape-shifter of some sort?" Eve suggested.

"There is a Japanese frog, Rana rugosa, that has both

XX and XY chromosomes and can change sex at will. So it is not unheard of in the natural world," Caine explained.

Hector ran a shaky hand over his face. "Are you suggesting that our perp can change from a male to a female and back again at will?"

Caine didn't respond, just arched his brow. But Jace knew what that meant. The chief definitely considered that a possibility. One they should seriously look into. But if it were true, it posed too many problems to even think about. This whole time they were operating on the assumption that they were looking for a male suspect, when in fact they could be looking for a female one. A suspect who couldn't logically exist.

Before anyone could respond, there was a knock at the door. Hector, who sat nearest to it, opened it. One of his assistants stood nervously in the doorway. He didn't look in, but kept his gaze on Hector.

"You better come outside, sir."

From out in the hall, Jace could hear a growing commotion of people. Several raised voices. One of them sounded like the sheriff. And he didn't sound happy.

Hector glanced over his shoulder. He looked unnerved. "I'll be right back."

When he was gone, Jace looked around at everyone. "I think our problems are about to get worse."

Caine shut the folder sitting in front of him and pushed it across the table. "I believe someone doesn't want us to solve this case."

Tala reached across the table and grabbed the folder,

dragging it over to her. It looked like she wasn't listening to the conversation, but Jace knew she was taking it all in. Her flickering gaze from team member to team member spoke volumes.

Eve sat up straight in her chair, her eyes wide. "Someone with power, do you think? Someone from our community?"

"I don't think it was a coincidence that my past has been revealed. I have gone to great lengths to bury most of my long life. It would be most improbable for a mere reporter with limited ability to find out the things she did."

"Someone tipped her off," Jace added.

Caine nodded. "That is my thought."

"Who?" Lyra asked.

"The baron," Jace offered. "It's no secret the two of you dislike each other."

Caine shook his head. "Laal is too much of a political animal to do something like that. He'd have to be gaining something in return and I just can't see what that could be."

Tala pushed her chair back, the rollers squeaking with the sudden movement. She held up Darryl Rockland's mug shot. "Did y'all see this?"

"What?" Jace asked, taking the picture from her hand.

She pointed to a dark mark, a bruise on the suspect's neck. "I've seen this mark before. On the teen that attacked me in the lot. He had a similar bruise on his neck."

Jace stared at the picture, trying to remember the youth on the ground. Had he seen something similar? The youth did have several bruises on him, but did it look the same?

Lyra stood and snatched the photo from Jace. "Let me see."

Everyone watched her as she studied the picture. Jace could see the twitch at her eye. Something was registering. And that something couldn't be good by the way her skin went deathly pale.

"It looks like a goat's head," she finally said.

It was as if the air had been suddenly sucked out of the room. Jace could smell fear floating off each of them. He was definitely missing something here. What did a goat's head have to do with anything?

"Okay, I'm obviously missing the punch line here. He has a bruise that looks like a goat. Why is that so scary?"

Lyra went to open her mouth, but Jace beat her to it. "And if you say anything about demons, I'm going to seriously rip something to shreds."

"Fine, I won't say it to you." Lyra turned and looked at Caine. "It's a demon mark. Meaning in service of."

Jace went to say something, but the door opened again and Hector returned. He shut it behind him and leaned on it for support. Jace didn't like the look on his face. It was one of impending doom.

"I'm sorry, my friends, there isn't anything I can do."

Jace glanced at Caine. The chief looked like he knew exactly what was coming.

With a sigh, Caine stood, grabbed Eve's hand and pulled her up with him. He put his arm around her. "You've done what you could, Hector, and I appreciate it."

Jace stood, too. But he was not as calm as Caine. "What the hell is going on?"

A hard knock came at the door. "Open up, Hector."

Hector turned the knob on the door and pulled it open. The sheriff stood framed in the doorway, his face a stoic mask. He marched in, six uniformed officers following in his wake. Each of them a bruiser in size.

"You're making a big mistake, sheriff," Caine said. "There are going to be more murders."

"The only mistake here is the one I made allowing Hector to call you in on this case," he answered. "I have the media and now the Kipfers breathing down my neck about your questionable background as a crime-scene investigator and your team members disappearing from crime scenes. As well as a kid in the hospital raving about werewolves." His hard gaze settled on Jace. "I should have you arrested for assault."

Jace could feel the man's animosity building around him. The acrid smell made him want to sneeze. But he was not about to back down.

"I didn't touch that kid. He's a gangbanger and was about to…" Jace paused when he met Tala's gaze across the room. She looked horrified. Her eyes pleaded with him not to reveal her secret.

He wished she believed that he would never even consider it. They had some serious trust issues to work out.

Jace shook his head. "The kid's a punk. He doesn't know what the hell he's talking about."

"Regardless of what's true or not. The media is

having a field day with it, bringing up that Liam Wolf and his stunt on TV, government cover-ups and conspiracies." His hands fisted tightly. "And I will not have this circus in my city. You are to vacate these premises and the city immediately."

Hector shook his head. "You should reconsider your decision, sheriff."

The sheriff turned his steely eyed gaze to Hector. "And you should reconsider how far you want to push me, Captain Morales."

Caine stepped forward and put his hand on Hector's arm. "Our presence isn't worth the fight, Hector. This lab's going to need your level head soon enough." He leaned into Hector's ear and whispered. "Don't trust anyone."

Jace was the only one that could hear every word.

As the officers rounded them up and escorted them down the hall to collect their crime-scene kits and personal effects, Jace looked for Tala. She was in the back, shoving her way through the pack of onlookers. Her gaze locked onto his.

He wanted to reach out to her, to touch her again. Already he could feel the loss of her body heat and her scent. He could actually feel their connection bending under the strain. His heart ached. He had never experienced that before. It hadn't even occurred to him that it could happen. Not now, not in this city of humans.

The mob stopped by the staff room and three more officers were there with their stuff. Anger swept through Jace at the notion that they hadn't even let them gather their own items. He was shaking with the thoughts of the officers going through their kits and taking things. It was a personal invasion. Something Jace thought he had left behind with the stinking freak show of his childhood.

As a group, they continued to move toward the main exit and the waiting vehicles to transport them back to Necropolis like common criminals. Or, worse, like animals.

Before they reached the door, Jace turned again and sought out Tala. She was there, following behind, trying to keep up but getting pushed around by the curious and the more sinister members of the lab and police that were enjoying the fiasco. Jace could smell their amusement. It sickened him.

Stopping in his tracks, Jace began to push his way back through the crowd toward Tala. An officer made a grab for him but Jace was too quick and too strong for him to get a solid hold on his arm. A low menacing growl rumbled from his throat as people stood in his way. The mob split open and allowed him access.

Tala pushed past the last two people and grabbed Jace's hands. He pulled her close and wrapped his arms around her, nuzzling his face into the silk of her hair. He could feel her vibrate under his touch and he knew she suffered as he did.

"I couldn't leave without touching you one last time," he murmured into her ear.

She dug her fingers into his back but said nothing. He felt her sudden intake of breath and knew she was stifling her tears.

He pressed his lips to her temple. "Find that boy. Get pictures of his mark. Make the connection. And trust no one."

They were torn apart. A burly officer held his arm. His other hand was on the butt of his gun. "Don't make me shoot you."

Jace grinned at him. "I could grab that gun of yours before you could even blink. Think twice about threatening me again."

The officer dropped his hand from his weapon and let go of Jace's arm.

Jace looked back at Tala. "Stay safe."

"You, too."

He turned around and allowed the officer to veer him back to the mob waiting for them near the front exit. Caine arched a brow when Jace got in place behind him. The vampire didn't have to say a word.

As they continued the procession toward the door a voice sounded beside Jace.

"Mr. Jericho! Mr. Jericho!"

Jace turned to see Rick running alongside the mass of people. He smiled at the young lab tech. His hair was sticking up all over the place; it looked like the guy hadn't showered in days.

"Mr. Jericho, I'm with you, man." He punched his fist into the air.

Jace shook his head and smiled. "Stay cool, kid."

When they reached the doors, the officers pushed everyone back as, one by one, Caine, Eve, Lyra and Jace exited the building and into the mass of reporters waiting outside. From one mob to another, Jace thought.

Maybe it was best that they were leaving San Antonio. Their presence was only causing more problems than they were solving. He knew it wouldn't work out. There was no way that Otherworlders and humans could work peacefully together. This just proved that he was right about them.

Sometimes being right just felt wrong.

Chapter 22

Elation and satisfaction filled him as he watched the members of the OCU being herded into the waiting SUVs by the human police. Pushed and shoved around like cattle. It was perfect.

He had risked being recognized by being out in the daylight, but he couldn't resist watching their humiliation as they were escorted out of the building and eventually out of the city itself. The dejected look on Caine's face and the rage on the lycan's were well worth the trip out.

They had been getting too close to the truth to allow them to continue their investigation. A few phone calls were all it took to turn the tide. Humans were so busy to manipulate. Power had its privileges. Something he had been reveling in for a long time.

If only they knew the true scope of his power. They would quiver from fear.

Some days he ached to reveal himself to Caine and his team of miscreants. He longed to see the flicker of horror and awe on their faces with the knowledge of his true identity.

But the ruse needed to continue for a while longer. He wasn't quite finished his work.

Three more to go until he could fully realize his purpose.

Once the vehicles pushed through the gathering crowd of reporters and curious onlookers, he moved on from where he stood on the fringe of the crowd. Walking down the street, he began to plan his next move.

As the sun waned in the distant sky, he smiled a little. Since it was such a beautiful day, maybe a stroll down by the River Walk was in order. He had time yet. Nightfall was the best time for hunting.

Chapter 23

Before Tala could make her escape from the police station to go to the hospital, the sheriff called her and Hector into a meeting.

She sat on one of the sparse wooden visitor chairs in the sheriff's office and waited for the chastisement she was certain was coming. Hector sat beside her, his leg jiggling up and down. He looked as nervous as she felt.

The sheriff sat on the edge of his desk and glared at them both.

"Due to the delicate nature and circumstances of this case I expect discretion from you both. I don't want either of you discussing this case with anyone here in the lab or outside of it. Remember the contract you signed about the Otherworlders. I will assign you both to new cases."

"Sheriff, may I speak?" Tala asked.

"No, you may not." He stood. "I expect all pertinent information and evidence either of you may have in this case presented to me immediately. Failure to do so will result in immediate release from your position."

"What if there is another murder, sir?" Tala couldn't keep her mouth shut; she was too angry. Something more was going on.

"That is no longer your concern." He rounded his desk and sat in his expensive leather chair.

"But, sir..."

"I told you to shut your mouth, Officer Channing. I suggest you do it immediately. You are already on shaky ground."

Hector put his hand on her arm. "Tala," he warned.

"Sir, I'm sorry, but I don't think you understand...."

The sheriff steepled his fingers together on his desk. "Officer Channing, if you speak again I will suspend you without pay. I will look into the allegations from the narcotics division of your possible involvement with drugs and also why you left the scene of a crime unexpectedly without informing Officer Vargas of your intentions or whereabouts." He leaned back in his chair. "And if you push me further, I will also look into the attack of the youth still in hospital care. I can't arrest your lycan friend, but I can arrest you."

Fury wrapped its strong arms around her as she

stood. It took all the control she had not to leap across the desk and wrap her hands around the sheriff's throat and squeeze until his doughy face turned purple. She always knew politics were at play here, but never to the extent that a murderer would remain free because of the incompetence of this office.

Her hands shook as she stood. "Am I done here?"

"You're dismissed, officer," the sheriff sniffed.

Tala turned and marched out of the office. As she strode down the hall to the parking garage, Rick jumped out at her from a darkened room. He grabbed her arm and tugged her into the storage room and, after glancing each way down the hallway, shut the door quietly behind her.

"What are you doing?" she demanded, shrugging off his grip.

"I think we should form a plan and a way to communicate without other people listening," he said.

"I have no idea what you are talking about."

"A plan," he said, his bushy brow arched, "to help Mr. Jericho and the team solve the strange murders."

"There is no plan, Rick. Jace is gone and we will be assigned to another case."

He nodded and grinned. "There is *always* a plan. Gwen and I have already discussed the logistics."

"Gwen?"

He smiled again and Tala could see the moony-eyed look on his face. "The brilliant lab tech from Necropolis. She's in agreement with me that we—you and me—

should continue to collect the evidence and smuggle it out to her."

Tala shook her head and went to open the door. "Rick, my advice to you is to stay out of it and do your job. The one you're told to do."

"Hey, do you think we should inform Hector of our plans? Or do you think he's a political liability?"

She opened the door and walked out. Rick followed her, still surveying the area as if he were a secret agent.

"What's our code word going to be?" he asked as he continued to trail her down the hallway.

When Tala reached the parking garage door, she yanked it open and looked at Rick, who was busy thinking about secret code words. She could tell by the way his forehead wrinkled and his eye squinted. "It's over. Let it go."

He glanced at her and smirked. "That's an awful code word." He patted her on the shoulder. "Don't worry, Tala. I'll think of something." He turned and shuffled back down the hallway. He waved his arm in the air. "The man cannot keep us down."

She watched Rick until he disappeared around the corner. Then she chuckled. She hoped he didn't spout off about his "plan" to anyone that mattered. The way the sheriff was going she wouldn't be surprised to see Rick on the unemployment line, standing right behind her.

She went into the garage and jumped into her vehicle. Before she started it, she sat and stared out the windshield. What was she going to do? The sheriff made it quite clear that he didn't want her anywhere near this ongoing case. But she couldn't just walk away. Not after everything they had gone through to get the evidence they had collected. Not after everything Jace and the rest of the OCU had tried to do. Caine had said there would be another murder and she believed him.

Maybe Rick had the right idea. Continue the search and keep gathering the evidence. What harm could come if she found the smoking gun and solved this case?

She'd be fired, that's what.

Maybe she could just pop in at the hospital and visit a sick kid. There was nothing wrong with that in the grand scheme of things. And the fact that she was going to buy a disposable camera along the way had no bearing on that visit at all.

The kid's name was Tommy Ross and he was on the sixth floor of the University Hospital.

When Tala reached the triage desk she flashed her badge and asked for his room number. The nurse at the desk pointed down the hall to room eight.

She wasn't quite sure what she was going to do once she got to his room. She couldn't just walk in and start snapping pictures of him, could she?

When she got to the door, it was propped open. She peered inside and saw Tommy asleep in a bed by the window. There was another bed in the room and it was occupied by a young black girl. Unfortunately, she was wide awake and saw Tala the moment she poked her head through the doorway.

Taking the plunge, Tala walked into the room, smiled politely at the little girl and continued on to Tommy's bed. As quietly as she could, she pulled the curtain around the bed separating them. She really didn't want a witness.

She took the disposable camera out of her jacket pocket and crept around to the other side of the bed. Tommy's head was tilted to the left so she'd have a perfect shot of his exposed throat. She noticed the dark mark instantly. It was situated on the lower part of his neck just above his lat muscle. It was blacker than a regular bruise. And by now, if it was just an ordinary bruise, it would've started to turn different shades of green or yellow. It did look like a goat's head. A long face with horns.

She snapped a couple of pictures of it. After the third take, Tommy started to stir. Time to go.

But before she could walk around the bed, he was fully conscious and making a lot of noise.

"You," he croaked, pointing a finger in her direction. "You're a…a…"

She rushed back around the bed and covered his mouth with her hand. Bending down to his ear, she said, "I suggest you be quiet. You wouldn't want to make me angry again, now would you?"

He shook his head, his eyes wide in terror.

"I just came to talk, Tommy," she said. "I have a couple of questions for you then I'll leave you alone. Do you understand?"

He nodded.

Slowly, she took her hand off his mouth and stepped away. Jace's words came back to her. *A human lie detector.* Reaching over, she took hold of his hand and wrapped her fingers around his wrist.

He struggled against her hold. "Let go."

"Don't worry, Tommy; I'm just taking your pulse. Like the nurses do." She smiled at him and he instantly stopped fussing. His heart was pumping but she knew it was out of fear.

"How did you get that mark on your neck?"

"What mark?" he sniffed, but his eyes didn't shift. It was human nature to try and look for the thing that another person was asking about, even if it was located in an impossible position to see.

With her other hand, she pressed her thumb over the mark. He winced. "This one."

He shrugged. "I don't know. I get bruises sometimes. No big deal."

His pulse spiked. He was lying.

"Do you know Darryl Rockland, otherwise known as Rock?"

"No."

Again his pulsed jumped. Another lie.

She leaned forward and let her lycan rise to the surface. Just a little. Enough that her eyes glowed. Without the silver nitrate rushing through her system, it proved easy to do.

"I know you're lying to me. And when I find out the

truth, and I will find out the truth, Tommy, I'm going to make sure that you are charged with accessory to two murders."

"I didn't kill no one," he sputtered.

"But I know you know who did." She squeezed his wrist tighter. His pulse was racing. "Give me a name. Something to go on."

"I don't know who killed those girls. I really don't."

His pulse was racing but it didn't spike. He was telling the truth about not knowing. But he still had information they could use to catch the killer.

"Tell me something you do know then, like how you got that mark. Darryl Rockland has the same one. Why?"

The look in his eyes was one of pure panic and fear. He was deathly afraid of something and Tala didn't think it was of her. Surely, she wasn't that frightening.

"A few weeks ago, I was partying with some friends. I took some drugs and passed out. I don't remember much after that, but when I woke up the next day I had this mark."

"There's something you're not telling me, Tommy. I can see it in your eyes. Who were you with? What did you see?"

He shook his head. "I don't know."

"Yes, you do. Think, damn it."

"A wolf. I think I saw a wolf. And the moon."

Flinching, she stared at him. "Are you sure?"

"Yes."

"Were you outside? In the woods?"

He shook his head. "I was definitely indoors. And I heard lots of noise. Music, I think."

"What else?"

"That's it. I can't remember anything else." Tears streamed down his cheeks. He looked as if he was going to throw up. "Now *his* voice is in my head."

"Whose voice?"

"I don't know. But he whispers to me. Tells me to do things." His eyes widened and fresh tears formed in the corners. "He told me to go after you in the parking lot."

She flinched at that confession. A phantom voice had spoken to him, told him to attack her. Who knew of her involvement in the case, besides those already on the case?

"Did you know the girls that were murdered? Did you seen them before?"

He shook his head and his pulse remained steady. He wasn't lying about that.

Tala let go of his wrist. "Tommy, you have an opportunity here to get yourself straight. I suggest you use it." Tucking the camera into her jacket pocket, Tala turned and walked around the bed to leave.

"Wait" he called, reaching out to her. "What should I do if I hear his voice again?"

"Don't listen to it. And get off the drugs. They're going to kill you."

Tala left the room with the intention of going back to the lab and finding Rick. They had work to do and little time to do it.

Chapter 24

Once the team trudged down the hallway to the staff room of Boneyard, Jace tossed his duffel bag onto the floor and cursed. Loudly.

"It's utter crap, Caine. Isn't there anything we can do?"

Caine moved to the sink, grabbed a teacup from the cupboard and filled it with water. After dropping in a teabag, he plunked it into the microwave. It was his custom when they started a shift. As the water heated, Caine rubbed a hand over his face.

His usual casual elegance was wearing down. With his tie askew and wrinkles in his usually pressed pants, he looked as tired and worn out as the rest of them. The case was taking its toll on everyone.

"What would you have us do, Jace?" Caine asked as he took out his cup of tea and sipped it. "Storm the gates? Take up arms?"

"So you're just going to give up? Let them win?"

"I'm not giving up, Jace, but I'm inclined to be more pragmatic about this than you are." Caine sighed. "I need a shower and a pint of blood and then we can sit down and think this through."

Eve crossed the room and wrapped her arms around Caine. Setting his chin on top of her head, he closed his eyes and hugged her back.

"Oh, I certainly need this," he murmured.

Jace turned away from the display. This was not the opportune time to be reminded of something he'd nearly had.

Pacing the room, Jace asked, "Isn't there a back door we can sneak through? Maybe Hector can give us a way in."

"Nobody from this lab is going anywhere." The baron's voice came from the doorway.

Jace turned around to see Laal, hands on hips, glaring. He looked pissed off.

"I've just been on the phone with Sheriff Atkins for the past hour. I'm ashamed to even repeat what he told me." Laal huffed. "All of you have disgraced this lab and this city with your unprofessional antics."

Caine moved so fast across the room that everyone had trouble seeing it, especially Eve, who was still righting herself from almost tumbling over from the sudden movement. He stood in front of Laal an equally angry—and more frightening—glare in his eyes.

"Don't even start, Laal. You have no idea what went on in San Antonio."

"I know enough—" Laal pointed a finger at Jace "—to consider arresting him. That poor boy may never get over what happened to him."

Jace snapped. It was instantaneous. He stalked across the room, grabbed Laal by the shirt collar and slammed him against the window of the staff room. The force of the impact cracked the glass.

"I could tear your throat out, bloodsucker."

Laal smiled and murmured quietly. "Not before I tore out yours, dog boy."

Caine was there in a second, pulling Jace off. The vampire was strong, but Jace had rage on his side and he remained pressed against the baron, his hands fisted in the fabric of his shirt. His teeth were starting to distend.

"Stand down, Jace," Caine demanded, his voice level but intense.

The power of it rippled over Jace's skin. Shivering, Jace let go of Laal and took a few steps back.

Brushing at the wrinkles in his shirt, Laal smiled again. But Jace could see a twinge of fear in the vampire's jaw and he could smell the ripe stench of it as it floated off him.

"You're fired," the baron stated. "Grab the stuff from your locker and get the hell out of my lab."

Jace made another run at Laal, but Caine stepped in

his way, pushing him back. He stumbled a few steps from the power of Caine's shove.

"Someone restrain him."

Jace wanted to laugh as Eve looked at Lyra and she looked at Caine. Like either one of them could restrain him. Then he spied Lyra's lips moving and her hand lifted out in front of her. Damn it! He didn't think she'd use magic on him.

Thinking he could run from it, Jace tried to make it to the door. But he couldn't move from where he was standing. The little witch had bound him to the spot.

She dropped her hand and shrugged. "Sorry, Jace."

Caine turned to Laal. "You can't fire him."

"Yeah," Lyra piped in. "He didn't even do what everyone says he did. Ta…"

Her words trailed off when she met Jace's glare. She pressed her lips together and slumped down into a chair.

The witch knew the truth. He could see it in her eyes and the way she looked at him. With sympathy and understanding.

"Oh, yes, I can," he sniffed. "I'm the baron here. Not you, Caine. It's best you remember that. I should fire you, too."

"Yeah, but you won't."

"Mistress Jannali thinks you're losing your edge. She thinks your team has become second-rate and would easily be replaced."

Caine leaned close into Laal's ear. "You can tell Ankara that she can shove it up her lily-white butt."

Jace laughed. "Yeah, tell her that from me, too."

"Me, too," Eve chimed in.

Lyra cleared her throat and squeaked, "And me."

The baron glanced at each of them, straightened his shoulders and walked to the door. Before leaving, he looked over his shoulder and said, "There is to be no contact with the human crime unit on this case or any case from now on. Break this and you'll all be looking for new jobs." Lifting his chin, he walked through the door and stomped down the hallway back to his office.

Caine turned around and rubbed a hand through his hair and sighed. "I think that went well."

Eve and Lyra chuckled, but Jace could hear the anxiety in the sound. He, too, felt trepidation. Maybe they had pushed the baron too far this time. He was certain that Mistress Jannali wasn't going to be pleased. And when she was angry the whole city shook with it.

"Could you release me?" Jace grunted.

Lyra lifted her hand and mumbled under her breath.

Within seconds, he could feel the pressure loosen and he was able to move again. He rubbed at his arms, still feeling the phantom tendrils of magic on his skin.

"Now do you have a plan?" Jace asked Caine.

The vampire arched a brow, a sure sign that he was formulating one. "Since they cleaned us out before we left, we need copies of all the evidence from the murders."

"How are we going to get that?" Lyra asked.

"Everything is downloaded into the computer system. Reports, crime-scene photos, witness statements. Everything," Eve responded with a gleam in her eye "And I can hack it all."

"Perfect." Caine moved to her and swept her into his arms. "My wife. The brilliant but diabolical computer wizard."

"I'll talk to my black arts contact and find out about this mark Tala was talking about," Lyra offered. "I'm also thinking we should go back through photos of Mel Howard and see if he had this mark, too. They have to be connected."

"Good thinking, Lyra," Caine said. "Let's get to work. I'll go and see Gwen and find out if she's made any headway on this mysterious DNA."

Jace stared at Caine. "And what am I doing?"

"You, my friend, are going for a long run. Chase off your pent-up anger and frustrations then go home and get some food and sleep."

"What?" He took a step toward Caine. "You're joking, right? You're actually going to let him fire me?"

"'Course not. But you aren't doing anyone any good the way you're acting." Caine sighed. "You are too edgy, Jace. More than usual. I don't know what happened between you and Tala, but you need to either get over it or deal with it."

"This isn't about a girl," Jace snarled.

Caine cocked that damn eyebrow again. "Isn't it?"

Cursing, Jace stormed across the room and out the door. Damn it, if the vampire wasn't right. He was edgy because of Tala, because he hated having to leave her. He had attacked the baron because he mentioned the teen that Tala had encountered.

Damn if the woman wasn't going to kill him. All the way from another city.

He had a feeling that going for a long exhaustive run wasn't going to dent the aggravation he was feeling. Only one thing could ease his frustrations. Unfortunately, what he had in mind was a little hard to do long-distance.

Chapter 25

By the time Tala ambled through the front door of her house, it was after one in the morning. Tossing her jacket and her shoes into a corner, she collapsed onto the sofa.

Exhaustion was trying to settle in. But the reserve of power humming through her refused to let it consume her. She'd never felt that sensation before and knew it was due to her lycan trying to free itself from the silver nitrate she'd been poisoning it with.

It had been close to twenty-four hours since she last dosed and she felt surprisingly in control. Maybe Jace had been right. Maybe she could learn to control it and use it to her advantage. He said her gift didn't have to be a liability. She was starting to believe him.

After her visit to the hospital, Tala had gone back to the lab intent on finding Rick and making plans to contact the OCU and get information to them, but she'd been intercepted by Captain Morales with another assignment. Technically, she was still on loan from narc.

For the past three hours she'd been running through hundreds of hours of surveillance video connected to an ongoing bank robbery investigation. It had been tedious and unsuccessful but it had afforded her an opportunity to copy the security footage from the second murder onto a disc. Now she'd just have to download it to her personal computer and she could send it to Jace.

She also had other unfortunate news to share with him. Another murder had occurred. The body was found and called in just as she was making her way out of the lab to go home. She deliberately ran into Rick on the way to the parking garage. He told her he'd pass on any information he could get. But the sheriff had reassigned him to other duties, too. Someone had seen him talking with Jace before they were ushered out of the lab and had ratted him out. There had even been chatter in the lab about Rick being a traitor. It was as if they were at war!

Her stomach rumbled. She put a hand over it and rubbed. She couldn't remember the last time she'd eaten. Standing, she wandered into the kitchen and opened the refrigerator door. There was nothing inside but week-old pizza. She took out the box, opened the lid and began chomping on a cold piece.

She'd eat, then call Jace. Maybe her stomach would stop flipping around once she filled it with food. Surely, she couldn't be this nervous about calling the lycan.

Concentrate on the case, not the man!

This was proving to be more difficult than Tala realized. Since his departure, she'd been feeling strange. Detached in a way. As if some phantom part of her had been removed. She hated the sensation. There had been a constant cool breeze blowing over her. Shivers had erupted over her skin and she'd had to resort to wearing her jacket in the lab. She hadn't been able to get warm. Even now, she quivered.

Maybe she was coming down with something. The only thing wrong with that reasoning was she'd never been sick. Not one day in her life. Once she went through puberty and realized what was stirring inside of her, she knew why. Lycans rarely got sick, if ever.

Stuffing the last of the pizza in her mouth, Tala wandered out of the kitchen to her computer desk in the corner of the living room. She sat at the desk, booted up her computer and slid the CD-ROM she'd made into her disc driver.

She picked up her cordless phone and punched in Jace's cell number. As it dialed, her hands shook and her throat tightened.

The phone rang six times before he answered. But when he did, those butterflies fluttering in her stomach quickly transformed into hummingbirds and made a descent to lower, more intimate regions.

* * *

Jace had just walked into his place, naked and sweaty from a four-hour run, when his cell phone trilled. Still raging with anger and frustration, he snatched the phone, intent on giving the caller an earful, until he heard her voice….

"It's Tala."

His heart leaped into his throat and he could barely form words. Her voice was like music in his ears. A sweet haunting melody that made his blood race and his body tighten.

"Hey," he finally managed to get out.

"Ah, I just phoned to let you know I have that security footage for you and some other stuff I managed to find out. Oh, and there was another murder," she said all in one breath.

Jace sat on his sofa and turned on his laptop. "Okay, send the info to my e-mail address." He told her the address, and as he opened his mail server he could hear her typing and the whir of her disc drive. He imagined her sitting at her desk, her hair unbound and falling around her shoulders, looking tired but pumped about something. He wondered what she was wearing.

Mentally, he slapped himself in the head. He had it bad if he was trying to envision what she had on while waiting for her to send him important information about a murder case. Still, his mind remained on that even as new mail popped into his in-box.

"Did you get it?"

Jace clicked on the new message. It was a short note with an attachment. "Yeah, thanks." He clicked on the attachment. Streaming video popped up. Instantly, he recognized the elevator from Rebecca's apartment building. "Looks good."

"I saw the kid in the hospital. His name is Tommy Ross and he's involved somehow. The mark on his neck is definitely not a bruise. But he doesn't remember how he got it. Just ramblings about a wolf, a moon and a voice in his head." She sighed. "I don't know. I think the kid's taken too many drugs."

Jace filed away the information she just gave him. "What about the newest murder? Anything?"

"No. I've been reassigned and warned to stay as far away as possible from the case." She chuckled softly. "But your inside man says he's going to do what he can to get me something to go on."

Jace laughed. Rick, the geeky lab tech, was his inside man now? Scary thought. "He's a determined fellow."

She joined in his laughter. "That he is."

"Have they picked up Darryl yet?"

"No. He's disappeared."

Sighing, Jace leaned back against the sofa cushions. What he really wanted was to lean back into the comfort of Tala's arms and feel the soft rise of her breasts next to his skin. So vivid was the thought that he started to get hard.

Clearing his throat, he asked, "How are you doing?"

"What do you mean?"

"I mean how are *you* doing? Did you take any more silver nitrate?"

She paused and he could hear her breath. She was considering something. Probably whether to tell him the truth or not. "No."

He smiled. "Good. How do you feel?"

"I feel okay."

"Tala, I can tell by the rise in your voice that you're not telling me the whole truth and nothing but the truth."

"Fine." She huffed. "I feel better. Stronger. Not as worn out or tired."

"You see, sometimes I know what I'm talking about."

"I guess."

By the way she spoke, he could tell that she was smiling. Warmth spread over him. Up from his toes across his torso and to his head. At this moment, Jace was very thankful he wasn't wearing any clothes. Lots of room for him to grow. Which he was doing rather quickly with her breathing in his ear.

"Miss me?" he asked.

"No," she sputtered.

"Yes, you do. I can tell in your voice."

"Bull."

He laughed. God, he wished he could see her face. His gaze roamed over his laptop and to the contraption attached to it. He leaned forward. "Hey, do you have a webcam?"

"Yeah, why?"

"Because I want to see you."

There was a sudden intake of breath. He loved hearing her do that.

"We don't need to see each other to talk about the case."

"Girl, for what I had in mind, it would certainly help if I could see you."

"Jericho. I'm hanging up now."

He chuckled. "I love it when you sound all shocked and righteous. Makes me as hard as stone, sugar."

She paused. But he could hear the sudden spike of her heart rate. He hoped she was imagining what he looked like hard as stone.

"Jace, this can't go anywhere."

"What can't?"

"You and me."

It hurt hearing her say that, but Jace knew she did it out of reflex to protect herself. Something she'd been doing her whole life to keep people away, at arm's length. He could accept that separation. For now.

"Tala, it's just a webcam. It's not forever. Turn it on and let me see you."

There was a long pause and for a brief moment he thought she was going to refuse and hang up on him. But after a few agonizing minutes, she agreed.

Setting the phone down, Jace turned on his webcam, tilted it toward his face—he didn't want to frighten her with his nakedness—signed into IM and waited for Tala. A minute later, a message popped up and there she was. Her striking image flickered on his screen.

She was frowning. And she looked absolutely adorable doing it.

He smiled. "There you are, gorgeous," he said into the built-in microphone on his computer.

The corners of her mouth twitched. Immediately, she rubbed a hand over her mouth to camouflage it. Too late, he thought.

"This feels absolutely juvenile."

He chuckled. "I know, ain't it great?"

As she laughed her eyes dipped lower and her smile faded. "Are you naked?"

He glanced down at himself and his growing erection. "Yup. I sure as hell am."

He could see her cheeks pinken. He loved it when she acted so embarrassed. It made him want to do things to outrage her, just to see her reaction.

"You're a pervert, you know that?"

"I know." He leaned back against the sofa. "And you love it."

"I don't."

"Oh, yes, you do." Jace set his right hand down in his lap. He would show her just how perverted he could get. He wrapped his hand around his erection and began to stroke it nice and slowly.

Again her gaze dipped low. She flinched but he could see the way her eyes narrowed and could hear the slight increase in her heart rate and breathing.

"Jace, I can see your arm moving. You better not be doing what I think you're doing."

"I am, babe. But I sure wish it was your hand touching me." Jace increased his rhythm. Already, he was very close to coming. Just knowing that Tala was there watching him made him burn inside and out. "Join me."

"What?" she sputtered.

"Come on. You don't even have to get naked. Just unbutton your pants and slide your hand down."

She shook her head. "No way." But the flush on her face was telling him she was certainly enticed by the thought.

"I'd love to watch your face as you touch yourself, Tala. I can't imagine anything as sexy as that."

He watched in fascination as her resolve broke. She began to unbutton her blouse.

"This is crazy, you know that, right?"

He nodded, his throat too constricted with blossoming desire to get out any words. By the way his mind was muddled, he was sure the words wouldn't make sense anyway.

Once Tala's shirt was undone, she parted the halves. She was wearing a simple white cotton bra, but it nearly did him in to see her in it. The tops of her breasts quivered when she breathed. He wished he could lick her skin right along the V of her breasts.

Her right hand disappeared below his line of vision on the screen. But he didn't need to see what she was doing. It was written all over her face.

The hesitation and then the heightened desire as she unsnapped her pants and slid her hand into her panties. He could picture it in his mind and it nearly made him groan.

He watched as she shifted in her chair and this time he did moan. He imagined her spreading her legs to accommodate her fingers. Was she sliding them over her slick flesh, trying to find that perfect spot? The one sensitive place that would send her reeling and out of control.

Her breathing quickened in his ear through the microphone. If he listened closely, he could discern the liquid sounds of her fingers moving over her body. Gritting his teeth, Jace slowed his pace. He didn't want it to be over too soon.

He wanted this to last as long as it could. Because he feared not seeing her again. Not in the flesh, not onscreen, not in any form.

"Oh, um," she panted. "I've never done this before."

"Me, neither." His body was nearing orgasm. Every muscle was tightening, getting ready to snap. But he wanted to wait until she was close.

When she tossed her head back and gasped, he bit down on his lip. She was so sexy, so utterly beguiling. He wished with all his heart that he could be there with her, touching her, making her squirm and gasp his name over and over again. Nothing would please him more.

"You're so damn beautiful, woman," he groaned. "I wish I could touch you."

"You are touching me, Jace." She moistened her lips with her tongue. "These are *your* fingers on me, inside of me. It's you. Only you."

He increased his pace, stroking himself hard and fast. He could barely breathe as the first flutters of orgasm rippled over his thighs and squeezed other parts of his body. Clamping his eyes shut, he reached for his discarded T-shirt and, wrapping himself tight in it, he came hard.

Tala's moans of pleasure echoed in his ears.

Opening his eyes, he watched as she came. Throwing her head back, she squeezed her eyes shut and opened her mouth, ragged breaths coming hard and fast. She was lost in her orgasm and he loved watching every moment of it.

Finally, she opened her eyes. "Oh, my."

He chuckled. "You could say that again."

"Oh, my." She laughed.

Tossing his shirt aside, Jace leaned toward the computer. He wished like hell that he could kiss her. He'd never felt a pair of lips as soft as Tala's. She was everything he ever wanted in a woman and more. Strong, passionate, caring and driven. And the most enchanting creature he'd ever seen. He was falling head over heels in love with her. He couldn't deny it any longer.

"Come to Necropolis," he blurted out.

Her smile faltered a little. "What?"

"You can get on the force here, no problem. They're looking for good cops."

"You want me to move to Necropolis?" She ran a shaky hand over her hair.

"Yes," he said, now desperately eager for her to listen. "You have nothing there for you, Tala. And everything here waiting for you."

"I can't just leave."

"Why not?"

She shook her head. "It's not possible, Jace."

"Yes, it is. You're just scared. It's understandable. But I'm here for you. I can help you with the transition."

She shook her head again. "No. I can't."

"*Won't* you mean."

"Doesn't matter." She sighed, and then began to re-button her blouse. "I'm sorry. You're asking me for too much."

"Tala…"

Without another word, she disconnected the video feed. Her face disappeared from his screen.

"Don't go," he said, too late.

With an angry sigh, Jace pounded his fist into the sofa. Damn it! He wouldn't let her push him away. He was too stubborn to go anywhere. He was like an animal that had a taste of blood. One taste was not enough. He was planning on a lifetime, whether she liked it or not.

Chapter 26

Jace streamed through the security videotape again. Rubbing a hand over his face to chase fatigue, he rewound to a few hours before the victim entered the elevator. There had to be something he was missing. The girl came home at around eleven and ended up tortured and murdered a few hours later. How did the perp get to her? Maybe he had already been in her apartment. If so, he had taken the stairs to get there and to leave. Because Jace couldn't find the bastard on the security tape. Unless what he was looking for wasn't registering.

Caine tapped on the door to the analysis room as he leaned against it. "Any luck?"

Jace shook his head. "I've been through it four times. Back and forth. Forth and back. Nothing."

"If there's something to find, I trust you'll find it."

Jace appreciated Caine's faith in his abilities. And he knew the chief had risked a lot by calling him back to the lab. If the baron found him, shit was going to hit the fan all over again. He was really too worn out to go through that once more. His heart wouldn't really be into the butt kicking he'd have to give the baron. No, his heart was somewhere else entirely right now.

"Have you gone through the rest of the evidence Eve was able to download?"

Caine nodded. "Yeah. Went through it all. We know he uses the drugs, maybe even the promise of sex, to lure the victims. So despite the double chromosomes, I'm betting we're still looking for a male. The key is knowing where our perp is finding his marks."

"Darryl was definitely part of the where."

"I agree. It's too bad he's just a shimmer in the wind now."

"You might have something there." Jace frowned and swiveled back around to stare at the video on his computer screen. Shimmer. There was something about it that made his pulse jump. Maybe the thing he was missing was the thing he *couldn't* see.

Caine came into the room and stood behind his chair. "You thought of something."

"No, you did."

"I did?"

"Yup." Jace forwarded the security feed to the time when the girl entered the elevator. Once the doors opened and she walked inside, he froze the image and stared at it.

"What are you looking for?" Caine asked.

"A shimmer." Jace traced a finger on the screen near the woman's side. "You see this." He pointed to a blurred spot. "I thought it was just a flaw in the video feed, but now I'm not too sure." Adrenaline started to surge through Jace. He was on to something. He could feel it. "And you see how she's standing? Kind of slumped over, like a puppet with slack strings."

"Yeah, I see that. Doesn't look natural."

"I think she's drugged and is being held up by someone else." Jace leaned back in his chair and ran a hand through his hair.

"An invisibility spell?"

"Yeah. We're looking for someone who definitely knows his magic."

Caine took out his cell phone and punched in a number. "Wake up. We need you down in the analysis room." He flipped the phone closed and slid it back into his pocket.

"This case is getting worse by the minute. We likely have a perp that can change gender at will, has claws and knows spells that only tier-one witches have mastered."

Jace nodded. "It's beginning to look that way."

Lyra bounded into the room, her hair falling out of her ponytail. "What? I was having a really great dream, you know."

"Can you determine magic from a picture?" Caine asked.

"Yeah. Probably. I can see magic as well as feel it."

"How about from a video feed?" Jace said, then pushed back his chair and stood to make room for Lyra.

She sat, shuffled forward and stared at the computer screen.

Anticipation thrummed over Jace's skin as he watched Lyra rewind the video and watch it play through. He sensed that he was right. They were dealing with something that outreached their usual scope. Maybe they had finally encountered a crime they couldn't solve.

"There's definitely a spell here." She pointed to the same spot that Jace had. "This shimmer is definitely a sign of spell casting. It looks red to me." She moved her finger around the victim's body. "It's all around her. It's some kind of cloaking spell. I've heard of them, but don't know anyone that can do one."

She leaned back in the chair and glanced at the ceiling. Shaking her head, she sighed. "Okay, okay. I'll tell them." She stood and glanced at Jace and Caine. "Gran says she can do one. But I personally have never seen it done."

Jace sat once more in the chair and looked at the screen. "If we fiddle with the video, do you think we can see past the shimmer?"

"I don't know. Might be worth a shot," Lyra responded.

"We can try different image intensifiers and see what

we get. Normally the image intensifiers are used through lens and tubes, but I've been working on a way to use the same technology to enhance video and photos by using infrared and night vision." Glancing over his shoulder, Jace motioned to Caine. "Turn off the lights."

Caine did and then shut the door. Except for the light flickering from the computer screen, they were shrouded in darkness. Jace zoomed in on the glimmer spot, enlarging it on the screen. Using a few key strokes, he was able to project the image through a different lens, as if he were using a camera with infrared capabilities.

Now they were looking at a different picture. An image that only projected heat signatures. And he could actually discern a form beside the victim in the elevator.

"That's amazing," Caine said as he leaned over Jace's shoulder. "That's definitely a body."

"Can you zoom out, Jace?" Lyra asked.

"Do you see something?" Jace asked her as he pulled back on the video image.

"Stop." She pointed to the screen. "What does that look like to you?"

Squinting, Jace peered at the image. He tilted his head until his eyes got a bead on the picture. It looked like a dark circle and something in the middle of it. Was that part of the perp's body? Or maybe what he was wearing.

"He's got a logo on his shirt," Jace blurted out.

"Looks like the moon to me," Lyra said.

Something clicked in Jace's mind. "Would you say that looks like a wolf howling to the moon?"

Lyra nodded. "Yeah, could be."

"Tala told me that the kid that attacked her said something about a wolf and a moon, and lots of music the night he got his mysterious mark. Maybe he saw this guy's T-shirt."

"Wait a minute." Caine rushed out of the room. A minute later he was back with a crime-scene photo. It was a picture of the second victim's apartment. He held the photo beside the computer screen. "I'd say that's the same image."

In the photo was a pack of matches. On it was a wolf howling inside a giant moon. Underneath that were the words *Howl at the Moon, Piano Bar, San Antonio*.

"I'd say we finally have a lead," Caine announced.

"Looks like it." Jace turned on his chair to look at Caine. "But how do we follow it?"

The chief smiled. "I'll think of something." His cell phone took that moment to ring. Sliding it out from his pocket he answered. "Valorian."

After a few head nods and arched brows, Caine flipped the phone closed and sighed. "But in the meantime, it looks like you and I have other matters to attend to, Jace."

"Like what?"

"We have been summoned to Mistress Jannali's office."

"What do you think she wants?"

Caine smiled, but it didn't make Jace feel any better.

Chapter 27

The mistress's outer office was as finely decorated as any royal castle. Not that Jace would really know what that would look like.

He stood along one wall and studied a painting hanging above him. The signature said Monet and he had no doubt it was authentic. From what he knew of Mistress Jannali, she didn't do copies. She had once been royalty in the Egyptian courts…the ancient Egyptian courts.

She was one of the wealthiest Otherworlders and most likely one of the richest people in the United States. Everything she owned reeked of old money. Her offices were no different. Except Jace smelled something else wafting through the room…arrogance.

This was the first time he'd been summoned to her office. He certainly hoped it would be the last. The place made him nervous. It felt like a mausoleum to the past.

Swiveling around to look at Caine, who lounged seemingly comfortably on the red leather chaise, Jace frowned. "How long is she going to make us wait?"

"As long as she wants."

"We've been here an hour already."

"I know, Jace, but you are aware that vampires, especially vampires as powerful as Lady Ankara, play by different rules."

"Yeah, yeah," Jace said, then sat down next to Caine on the sofa. "I know all about archaic vampolitics."

"Then you know to shut up and be patient."

"How can you be so calm?"

"I have to be to get us out of whatever we're certainly going to get into."

The doors to the inner office opened and a tall spindly man stepped out. "The mistress will see you now."

Caine then Jace went through the open archway and the man closed the doors behind them. A shiver rushed over Jace's spine when the click of the doors echoed around him. It felt so final. Like a lid closing on a coffin.

The office was huge but crammed with furniture and art. In an instant, Jace felt claustrophobic. He nearly bumped into Caine as he looked up at the sweeping, elegantly painted ceiling.

"Lady Ankara, it is a pleasure to see you again." Caine bowed his head.

Jace did the same but didn't speak. Because they were operating under vampire politics, he would only speak when spoken to by the hostess. He thought their traditions and customs were stupid, but then again, there were certain protocols to follow when addressing the alpha of his pack. Protocols he was sure others would find just as ridiculous. So he kept his mouth shut, even though he seriously wanted to speak about the case, the baron and other things he'd been noticing lately.

Mistress Jannali stepped out from a shadow in the room and into the light, returned Caine's bow and smiled. "It has been too long, Caine. You are surely missed at the club."

She was not what Jace had been expecting. He had heard of her beguiling beauty but was not prepared for the reality of it. She nearly took his breath from his lungs.

She was tall, regal, with a long, lean form draped seductively in an ocean-blue gown that swept the floor. Her skin was the color of cinnamon and looked just as delectable. The tips of her long, flowing black hair flirted at her slim waist. But it was her eyes that commanded attention. They were an unusual shade: lavender.

She turned those lavender eyes on him and he could feel the power thrumming through her. It was nearly overwhelming and he had to divert his gaze.

Glancing back at Caine. "How is your…woman?" She smiled. "I'm sorry I couldn't have attended your wedding. I had pressing matters to attend to overseas in Nouveau-Monde. I'm sure it was a lovely ceremony, though."

Caine inclined his head. "It was. Thank you."

"Did you get my gift? The lifetime membership to the club?"

Jace heard Caine grit his teeth.

"Yes. It was very thoughtful. Although I'm not sure Eve would be comfortable there."

"Doesn't she play racquetball?"

Caine shook his head. "I'm afraid not."

"Oh, that's too bad," Ankara remarked, smiling. "I was looking forward to playing with her. Oh, well, please give my regards to her then."

"I will."

"Please sit." She swept her arm toward four high-backed chairs arranged around a small circular table. A platter with a teapot and two cups sat waiting.

Jace followed Caine and sat in the chair beside him. Ankara took the chair opposite Caine on the other side of the table. She leaned over and poured the tea. She handed Caine a cup and saucer.

"Thank you," he said.

Ankara handed Jace his drink. He took it and nodded his thanks. He hated tea, but would drink it to be polite. He didn't want to offend her. Not yet, anyway.

Sitting back in her chair, she crossed her legs and picked up a silver cigarette case. She took one out and lit it with a match, letting the smoke slowly curl out from between her lips. The smell of sulfur floated to Jace's nose.

"Laal has informed me of the troubles your team had in San Antonio."

Caine set his tea down on the table. "Yes, I believe that my background was leaked to that reporter."

Ankara's eyes narrowed. "Are you accusing someone?"

"Not yet," he responded. "But I will soon enough."

The temperature in the room dropped a few degrees. Jace looked at Caine. The chief's jaw was twitching and Jace could smell the fury rising from him like smoke from a fire.

Jace turned his gaze onto Ankara. She was looking at Caine, studying him, as if considering him a little more seriously than before.

Then her gaze shifted onto him. Flinching, Jace nearly dropped his cup of tea.

That brought a smile to Ankara's lips. "And you, Jace Jericho, how do you explain your actions in San Antonio?"

"I'm not sure I follow you, Lady Ankara."

"Oh, I'm sure you understand exactly what I'm asking." She tilted her head, a ghost of a smile still on her lips. "Getting involved with a member of the San Antonio police force, losing a suspect, leaving a crime scene to go elsewhere…do I need to go on?"

Leaning forward, Jace set his drink on the table. His hands were beginning to shake. "Officer Channing and I are not involved."

"I understand that she's about to be suspended from duty pending drug charges. Maybe she knew who the suspect was because he's *her* dealer. Maybe she's your leak. She would've known about all of you before she was assigned to the team."

Jace exploded from his chair. "Tala is not involved with Darryl Rockland. She's a good cop."

"Laal was right about your temper," Ankara sniffed. "You are far too emotional to be a crime-scene investigator."

"Sit down, Jace," Caine ordered.

Although vibrating with rage, Jace sat as instructed. He desperately wanted to launch across the table at Mistress Jannali, but knew she was so powerful that ending his life would take but a minute. And he had a feeling that she wouldn't hesitate. He didn't think she shared Caine's ethics and morals when it came to bloodletting and killing.

She didn't become mistress of the city because of her popularity with the people.

"The baron is the emotional one in this case, Mistress. He is constantly hovering around my team, instigating conflicts and taking every little thing much too personally."

Ankara watched Caine silently, her eyes narrowed, her lips pressed tightly together. Then she smiled. "You're right, Caine. Laal is overly sensitive. Sometimes he's like a child, I'm afraid to admit." She nodded. "I will overlook the past transgressions of you and your team. The lycan can keep his job."

Caine stood and said, "Thank you, Lady Ankara."

Jace followed suit but didn't thank the vampire. He didn't think he could form the words. She disturbed him on more levels than he could even describe.

After a quick bow, Caine made his way toward the

door. Jace was right on his heels, eager to be out of the office and away from the mistress.

"Oh, and Caine," she said.

The chief stopped and glanced over his shoulder at her.

"Keep him on a short leash." She pointed at Jace. "And please don't contact Captain Morales in San Antonio or anyone in his lab. From now on, I will be the only one that deals with the humans."

Jace took a step forward, but Caine's hand on his arm stopped him from going any farther. He could feel the vampire's power pulsing through Caine's palm.

"Of course, Mistress." Caine bowed his head again. "Thank you for seeing us."

Keeping his hand on Jace, Caine moved toward the double doors. They swung open and Caine and Jace walked out together. Once through, they shut on their own accord, as if blown by a phantom wind.

As they walked to the elevators, Caine glanced at Jace. "What do you think?"

"I think Mistress Jannali is not your typical vampiress."

"Why do you say that?"

"I couldn't smell anything from her. Nothing. Not even when she got angry."

The elevator door chimed and opened. They walked on. Caine pushed the parkade button. "Trust me, she wasn't angry. I've seen angry and that wasn't even close to being it."

"I don't know. There was something off about this whole meeting."

"I agree. Like a little show me yours, I'll show you mine."

Jace shivered again. A sense of dread surged over him like a shadow casting across the ground. "Yeah, and I don't think we got to see hers at all."

Chapter 28

When Tala returned to the police station there was a message waiting for her at the front desk.

It read: *I have the last season of* The X-Files *on DVD if you want to watch it. R*

Shaking her head, Tala headed down to the lab. Rick wasn't really any good at this undercover stuff. She'd tell him to back off and stop with the supersecret snooping around. He was just going to get himself fired.

After a few long hours of thinking time, she came to the conclusion that she didn't want to get involved anymore. It was risking too much. Her job for one. And her way of life. She didn't want to sacrifice either. At least that's what she kept telling herself.

She found Rick in his lab, dancing to a Justin Timberlake song. He spotted her after a rather impressive spin around on his right foot and grabbing of his groin.

"I see you got my note," he said. "Pretty clever picking the *The X-Files*, don't you think?"

She shook her head. "Not really. I bet everyone that read this message knew exactly what you were talking about. It's not really a big secret anymore, Rick."

He shrugged. "Anyway. I found out that the third murder is very similar to the Kipfer one. The victim was found strung upside down, this time in a secluded park. Her throat was slashed, blood gone, the same symbols written in blood were on her chest. No witnesses. She was found by a late-night jogger." He frowned. "Who jogs at night?"

"Drugs?"

He nodded. "Yup, the same. MDMA."

"Was she raped?"

"No evidence of it. No semen present."

Tala sighed and rubbed two fingers over the bridge of her nose. A headache was threatening to explode behind her eyes. "Okay. Thanks, Rick, for the info. But no more. Don't risk your job for this. We are not undercover agents for the OCU."

He smiled appearing wistful. "If only."

"I've got to get back to work." She walked to the door. "I'll see you around."

"Oh, you might be interested to know that the sheriff doesn't know what to do."

"Doesn't surprise me," she muttered.

"And Captain Morales is trying to convince him to bring back Mr. Jericho and the rest of the OCU."

Now that did surprise her.

She waved at Rick and left. Walking down the hall, she pondered the information he gave her. She wasn't surprised that the MO was the same. After all she'd learned since Jace and his team had arrived, nothing much surprised her. The murders were linked, that much was obvious. They needed to track down Darryl Rockland. She was certain he would lead them to the killer.

She bumped into another person walking the opposite way and it knocked her from her thoughts. Tala apologized and kept on her way, but then she glanced up and realized she had walked all the way to the sheriff's office.

The door was closed, but she could hear raised voices behind the wood. One of them was the sheriff's and the other belonged to Hector.

She wanted to press her ear to the door to hear the whole conversation. But then she realized that she didn't have to do that. If she concentrated hard enough, she could hear everything going on in the neighboring offices.

Sitting in one of the benches along the wall, Tala turned her head just enough that she could literally tune in to the sheriff's office.

"Let me bring back Caine on this, sheriff," Hector said.

"No. I will not have those people in my lab or in my city. They are much too dangerous."

"The dangerous thing is not to involve them. They

know more about what's killing these women than we will ever know."

"Darryl Rockland is our murderer, Hector."

"I think you're wrong. He's involved, certainly, but I don't think he's our killer."

"I do. The Kipfers want someone to pay for their daughter's murder and I'm going to make sure that they get that compensation when we catch Rockland."

"You're making a huge mistake, sheriff."

Tala could hear the sheriff's angry intake of air.

"You're treading on shaky ground, Hector. Push me and I will push back. And I don't think you'll like where you'll end up."

Another minute ticked by, then the door to the office opened and Hector stomped out. He slammed the sheriff's door behind him and looked at Tala. She jumped to her feet.

He marched over to her. "What are you doing here?"

"Ah, waiting for you?"

He smiled. "Good. I was hoping I'd see you. Walk with me." Turning, he moved down the hallway to the elevators. She matched him stride for stride.

"Where are we going?"

"To meet our team. Our real team. We have a killer to catch. And I have no faith that the sheriff will catch the right one."

"I won't do it," Lyra said.

Jace glanced at Caine, who was sitting behind his

desk, and shrugged. He'd known that Lyra would argue. He would've been surprised if she had agreed.

"Lyra, we need this. It's important," Caine stressed.

"You are asking me to go against my morals, Chief."

"I know that, and I'm sorry. But it is really the only way that we can get back into San Antonio and solve this case. If we don't, more people will die, I have no doubt about that."

Jace watched Lyra as she fidgeted in her chair. He could almost see the wheels turning in her mind.

"Damn it, Lyra, just ask her. It's not as if she's using her powers."

Lyra turned around and glared at Jace. "I'd watch what you say about Gran. You know better than most what happens when you make her angry."

He did know. To this day, he still got the shakes and visions of zombies when he came near cemeteries. But he'd risk that to get a chance to follow a lead and have another opportunity to catch a killer.

"Ask her," Jace demanded.

She huffed. "Fine."

Caine stood. "Thank you." He rounded the desk and offered her his hand. She took it and he pulled her to a stand. "I owe you one."

She smiled smugly. "Yes, you do. There's a seminar in Nouveau-Monde France I want to attend."

"You got it."

"And I want a two-thousand-dollar bonus when I go so I can do some shopping."

Caine smiled. "It's yours."

"Hey, what do I get for all my work on this case?" Jace asked.

"My undying gratitude, as always, Jace." Caine moved toward the door of his office. As he left, Jace and Lyra followed. "Okay, let's move out. The car will be waiting for you at the east checkpoint."

Jace grabbed his arm. "You're not going?"

"It's best I stay. Laal will become suspicious if I'm gone."

They walked through the lab, grabbed an elevator up to the parking garage. Caine unlocked the door to one of the SUVs and tossed Jace the keys.

"You drive to the checkpoint, Lyra does the spell and the two of you jump the fence and make a run for it. I've been assured the car will be there a mile out on I-35."

"And if it's not there?"

"Then you run like the wind back to the checkpoint before the spell wears off and hope like hell that the guards aren't armed will silver bullets," Caine remarked as he patted Jace on the shoulder.

Despite the dire circumstances, Jace laughed. He couldn't help it. His adrenaline was running so high he felt like he needed to do something or he'd explode. Better now than when he was jumping the fence at checkpoint east.

Jace got into the vehicle, started it, and rolled down the window. He held his hand out to Caine. The chief took it. "We'll be back."

"I have no doubt." Leaning into the window, Caine said, "Lyra, take care of him."

She smiled and tipped her head. "Of course, don't I always?"

It took them a little more than twenty minutes to drive out of town to the checkpoint. As the lights of the government building came into view, Jace cut the headlights and coasted to a stop along the road.

He glanced at Lyra. "Are you ready?"

She nodded. Closing her eyes, she set her hands palms-down on her thighs and began to hum. Within seconds, her hums turned to murmurs. Then her murmurs turned to words that Jace couldn't decipher.

Another minute passed. Jace wasn't sure if what she was doing was going to work. But then a soft blue glow appeared above Lyra's head. As Jace watched the glow brighten, he swore he saw the haggard face of an old woman with flowing gray hair. She was glaring at him.

His body shook as tendrils of magic wrapped around his form, wriggling and squirming over his skin. The sensation nearly made him gag. Soon the whole vehicle was lit up with the blue light.

Jace felt smothered. He couldn't breath. Gran was trying to kill him, he was certain. She obviously didn't like to be made fun of. Reaching out, he grabbed on to Lyra's arm to stop her from completing the spell. It was too much. They'd find another way.

But then the light disappeared. And they were shrouded in darkness.

Jace had superior night vision but when he scanned the vehicle he couldn't see Lyra anywhere. Panic surged through him.

"Lyra?" He opened his car door and was about to step out, when something covered his hand. Jerking, he pulled from the touch.

"It's me, idiot."

Jace stared at the passenger seat. "Lyra?"

"Yes," she hissed. "It's an invisibility spell. What did you expect?"

"I don't know. I guess I expected to still see you."

"Well, you can't. Just like I can't see you." Her car door opened, then shut.

Jace slid out of the SUV and came around to the front. He could hear footsteps coming near him. He could also smell Lyra's floral scent.

He reached out and grabbed her hand. "We go together, then."

"Fine."

He pulled her to him, reached down, picked her up by the legs and hefted her over a shoulder. She was a tiny little thing, her weight insignificant.

She shrieked and started kicking. "What are you doing?"

"Shh, they'll hear you. I'm faster and stronger than you. It'll go a lot quicker if I just carry you over."

Her movements stilled and he heard her sigh. "Fine. I'm tired anyway. The spell wore me out." She slapped him on the butt. "Just don't drop me."

Chapter 29

Climbing the fence with Lyra over his shoulder took some strength and agility, but Jace was up and over within five minutes despite Lyra's muffled protests.

He ran full out along the side of I-35, prepared to jump into the ditch with any approaching headlights. Luckily, he didn't see any. After about a mile, there was an unmarked nondescript sedan parked along the left side. It had to be their car. *Thank you, Hector.*

"Our car's coming up," he whispered to Lyra.

"Then can you let me down, please?"

Stopping, Jace set Lyra on her feet. Well, he hoped it was on her feet, since he couldn't see her. And together they jogged the last little bit to the waiting vehicle.

When they approached, Jace could see one figure inside. Hector sat in the driver's seat, waiting. In the back of his mind, he had been secretly hoping that Tala would be there waiting for him, too.

Jace jogged alongside the passenger side and opened the back door. Hector turned in his seat, a startled look on his face. When the other back door opened, too, he jumped again.

"It's Jace and Lyra."

Hector laughed. "Damn. When Caine said you'd be invisible I thought he meant figuratively. You know, black clothing, camo face paint. Not *invisible.*"

"Well, that's the beauty of us. You never know what's going to happen," Jace remarked.

Hector started the car. "How long will the spell last?"

"Another half hour, tops," Lyra answered.

"Good. Because it's freaky talking to the air."

As Hector drove them back into San Antonio, he filled them in on the last murder and the hunt for Darryl Rockland. It was as if Darryl had vanished.

Jace informed Hector about what they had discovered on the security tape and ultimately what gave them the idea for the invisibility spell to get out of Necropolis.

What he really wanted to ask was about Tala. Jace needed to know that she was okay. No matter what happened, he would find the time to go see her. And hopefully convince her to return to Necropolis with him. This time, he refused to leave without her.

By the time Hector parked the car downtown, it was nearing 11:00 p.m. and the spell had worn off.

They got out of the vehicle and made their way down to the River Walk along the San Antonio river. It was crowded and noisy as entertainment seekers lined the stone walkways to gain access to the various bars and restaurants that occupied the area.

"The place we're going is called Howl at the Moon. It's a very popular piano bar. I myself have enjoyed a few nights out there. The wife loves it." He smiled then pointed to a building with a large blue-and-yellow sign down the side.

And standing out front near a tree was Tala.

Jace's heart sped up at the sight of her long legs wrapped in faded denim and the T-shirt and leather jacket she wore. Her hair was unbound and floated around her with the slight breeze.

She smiled when she spotted them and Jace thought his heart was going to rush into his throat. He wondered if it would always be this way when he saw her. A feeling of elation and excitement. He sure as hell hoped so.

Lyra elbowed him in the ribs, knocking him from his reverie. "Man, you got it bad."

"What are you talking about?" he growled.

"Just don't let it cloud your judgment."

Jace didn't have time to respond as they approached Tala. Her scent floated over him.

"Good to see you both," she said when they stepped up to her at the tree. Her gaze lingered on Jace.

He wanted to cross the short distance and gather her in his arms, pressing his nose into the silk of her hair. The urge to do so was so intense he had to dig his nails into his palms to stop from reaching for her.

"How long have you been here?" Hector asked.

"A half hour here out front. But for an hour I watched the place from over there." She pointed to a bench situated right along the riverbank. "I haven't seen Darryl or any tall single males going into the establishment."

"It's possible our new suspect works here or at least has been here in the last week or so," Jace said. "We should definitely go in and have a look around."

"Why don't we split up?" Hector suggested. "Two of us go in; two of us wait out here. Tala and I both have radios."

"Good idea." Lyra grabbed Hector's hand. "Let's go."

Before Jace could protest, Lyra and Hector were at the door to the bar and going in. Suddenly nervous, he glanced at Tala. She, too, seemed jittery. They were like damn teenagers and not two grown professionals doing their jobs.

"We should go sit over there." Jace motioned toward the bench Tala had pointed out earlier. "We'll pretend we're just out for a night stroll. On a date, like."

Nodding, she led him to the bench and sat. Jace sat beside her and put his foot up on his knee. Nerves sang through him as did adrenaline. He was ready, willing and able to get this guy. But a part of him was reluctant to finish the case. Because then he'd have to leave again. Now that he was with Tala, Jace never wanted to leave her side.

And he was going to tell her.

Keeping in line with the roles they were playing, Jace put his arm around her. As if leaning down to kiss her, he nestled in next to her ear. "Tala, there's something I need to tell you," he started.

Before he could continue, Tala wrapped her arms around him and pulled him close, nuzzling into his neck. "Suspect at three o'clock."

"What?"

"I said, I spotted the suspect at three o'clock."

Turning his head slightly, not wanting to leave the warmth of Tala's embrace, Jace watched as Darryl Rockland strolled past Howl at the Moon and went around the corner.

Tala released her hold on him and slid the radio out of her jacket pocket. "Suspect Rockland has been spotted. Heading east on Crockett Street."

The radio crackled. "Hold tight. We'll be there in two minutes."

Jace jumped to his feet. "This guy will be gone in two minutes." He walked toward the club. When he got to the door, he put his back to the wall and leaned around the corner. He saw Darryl duck into another building not far from where he was.

When Hector and Lyra met up with them, Jace said, "He went into another building about a block up."

"What's the plan?" Hector asked.

"This guy's a runner. He'll take off the second he gets wind of us."

"Then let's stay downwind," Tala said as she took point to lead them down the street.

Jace grabbed her arm. "Let me go first. I can track him easier."

She was about to protest, but her gaze flicked to Hector. He was staring at her, probably wondering why she would argue.

Nodding, she took a position behind him; Lyra and Hector followed Tala.

Lifting his nose, Jace scented the air. Almost immediately he picked up Darryl's odor. It was acidic, like vinegar. After he walked a block, the smell became stronger, concentrated. Turning, Jace faced an older brick building with storefronts. But above those were floors of large windows. Apartments above the stores?

Jace glanced at Hector. "Do you know this building?"

Hector shook his head.

Spying a painted door next to one of the shops, Jace turned the doorknob. It was locked. Getting a good grip, he tried again. This time, he squeezed the handle so hard, the lock popped off and he yanked open the door. The vinegar odor became even stronger.

"Hector, are you armed?"

"Yes."

"Okay," Jace glanced at everyone. "I'm going in first. Then Hector, Lyra and Tala."

"What if he's armed?" Tala asked. "You're not bulletproof, you know."

"No, but a lead bullet isn't going to take me down. I can take several shots before I'm out of the game."

Jace kept Tala's gaze. He could see the worry in her eyes and it made his heart swell. Grabbing her hand, Jace pulled her to him. She didn't object when he cupped her cheeks with his palms. "You'll not get rid of me that easy, woman."

"Good," she smiled.

Leaning forward, he pressed his lips to hers. It was quick but it was enough for now.

Letting her go, Jace glanced at Lyra. "Can you throw a binding spell?"

"Oh, yeah, no problem."

"Get one ready." He nodded. "Let's go."

Once Jace walked in he could see a set of stairs to his right. The tart odor wafted from down the stairs. Jace pointed his finger up, indicating the steps.

As they climbed to the second floor, a sudden wave of dread washed over Jace. Something wasn't right. It seemed much too easy finding Darryl when they did. Maybe they were lucky, being in the right place at the right time.

When they reached the second floor, Jace took a few steps down a short hall toward three doors. The vinegar smell intensified. And another odor came to him in a puff of stale air. Sulfur.

The scent was unmistakable.

Jace pointed down the hall. The others followed close

behind as he approached the first door. Setting his ear to the wood, he listened for any sounds inside. Nothing came to him except the hum of a heater.

He moved on to the next door. His eyes watered from the intense smell of vinegar and sulfur. Not the most pleasant combination. He set his ear to the door.

The sound of breaking glass sounded through the wood.

"He's there!" He yelled as he turned toward the door and kicked at it with his foot. One powerful boot to the lock, and the door burst open in a rain of splinters.

Jace rushed into the apartment just as Darryl ran toward the broken window.

"Lyra! Toss it!"

The witch burst into the room, hands out, murmuring under her breath.

The spell worked and Darryl froze in spot, his foot perched on top of the window ledge. Jace rushed him, grabbed his arm and tossed him backward. Leaning out the window, Jace spied a pile of shattered glass and a dark shape fleeing down the street. The scent of sulfur followed the suspect out.

"I'm going after him." Jace pulled his shirt over his head and tossed it to the floor. He looked at Tala as he undid his jeans. "Come with me."

She flinched. "What?"

"Shift and come with me. He'll never be able to outrun us both."

Her gaze flitted to Hector then back to Jace. "I don't know what you're talking about."

"Tala?" Hector moved toward her, concern wrinkling his brow.

"She's a lycan, Hector," Lyra announced.

Tala swung around and glared at Lyra. "You have no right."

Jace touched her arm, gaining her gaze. "I'm going. We can bring this guy down together."

"I can't," she bit out.

Jace stepped back and went to all fours. Without another word, he forced the shift through his body. Once transformed, he glanced at Tala again. Shame and regret flashed across her face. It speared his heart. Turning, he jumped out the window.

Chapter 30

As Jace rounded the corner of the building, the suspect was disappearing around yet another turn. The only thing that signaled the suspect's path were the screams that erupted in his wake.

When Jace took the next corner and rushed down the promenade, he could see the tail end of his quarry. Tail end was the operative word. He was quick on his feet and Jace now knew why. He was a lycan or at least had shifting abilities.

The suspect crashed through tables with umbrellas, mowing down everything in his path. Screaming patrons jumped out of the way. Some weren't lucky enough to move as fast and ended up in the river.

Jace followed the path of destruction. More screams erupted as he passed through. He could just imagine the news reports. *Killer wolves run rampant through the River Walk.*

For the next several city blocks, Jace followed the suspect's course. He ran as fast as he could, but he always seemed a little behind. Enough to still see the suspect, but not close enough to bring him down. A dangerous game of tag.

Veering off the path, the suspect jumped across the river. Jace bounded forward and nearly collided with a hot-dog cart. Coming to a stop, Jace turned and leaped across the water. On the other side, he lost sight of his quarry.

Still running, Jace followed his nose. The scent of sulfur permeated the air like a noxious gas. He jumped over a clump of shrubs. When he landed, he caught sight of the suspect crossing the road and heading toward an old stone building. The Alamo.

The suspect raced across the empty park and around another building corner. Jace chased him. He wouldn't give up until he had the guy in his teeth. Literally.

Rounding the corner of the building, Jace noticed it was an alley. What he didn't notice was that it was a dead end. He realized that a little too late….

The suspect stood crouching in a small pool of lamplight, waiting for him.

Jace skidded to a stop, nearly colliding with a large metal garbage bin. His quarry grinned when Jace came near him. Jace's skin crawled and the hair on his neck and back rose to attention.

The suspect was no lycan.

In the light, Jace could see that he wasn't covered in fur, but dark mottled skin. His muzzle was shorter, his eyes bigger and his canines much, much longer. More like a vampire's than a shifter's.

"Finally, it's just you and me, lycan," he snarled. "I've been waiting a long time for this moment."

Jace shook his head. Although muffled, the voice was familiar. The timber of it registered something in his mind. But he didn't even get a chance to grasp it before the suspect launched at him.

Leaping to the right, Jace swiped at his attacker. His talons ripped through the suspect's shoulder. Blood sprayed across Jace's flank. But it was as if Jace had never touched him. The suspect was up and around, leaping on Jace's back before Jace could even consider his next move.

Long thick claws dug into Jace's side, puncturing his skin and muscles. Pain ripped through his body and he had difficulty breathing. Had the bastard already punctured a lung with his long talons? He wouldn't let the fight be over so soon.

Shaking side to side, Jace managed to toss off the attacker. The suspect rolled across the alley and into the brick wall. Jace turned and leaped at him, intent on going for the guy's throat. But he was up and actually standing on his hind legs when Jace crashed into him.

His attacker wrapped his front legs around Jace like

a hug, squeezing him vise-tight. Jace snapped his jaws at the suspect's throat, but couldn't get close enough to get a grip. Turning his head, the suspect opened his mouth and bit down on Jace's muzzle. His long needle-sharp fangs pierced the top of Jace's nose and went into his lower jaw, sealing his muzzle shut.

Agony poured over Jace like an acid burn. Intense. Tearing. Burning. His eyes watered from the over-whelming intensity of it.

They rolled on the ground, locked in battle. Jace tried to yank his head away, not caring how much flesh he ripped out in the process. But the suspect had a steel grip on him. He wasn't going to get away. Not until the bastard was done with him.

Bringing up his back feet, Jace tried to push his attacker off. He tore and swiped at the guy's hind legs and lower extremities. But no matter how much damage Jace thought he was doing, the suspect did not relin-quish his hold on Jace.

As claws dug further into Jace's sides, he thought about Tala. He feared he'd never see her again. He had missed his chance to tell her how he felt. As blood ran down his flank and onto the cement, Jace wished she knew how much he was in love with her. How much he wanted her to move to Necropolis and start a family.

Finally, the suspect yanked his teeth from Jace's muzzle. But it was in vain to think that Jace could still use his jaws. They felt bruised and broken. He could barely open his mouth.

"And now it's time to die, Jace Jericho. Do you have anything you'd like to say?"

Jace wanted to scream, but instead, he reared his head back and lashed forward, smashing the guy in his face. He didn't think the move would work, but he had the satisfaction of feeling the hot spray of blood on his face and hearing a grunt of pain.

"You will pay for that." Lying on top of Jace, the suspect pulled out the claws from Jace's sides and lifted them high in the air. His eyes bugged out with fury as he brought them down toward Jace, intent on spearing his internal organs.

A streak of auburn dashed out of the shadows and rammed into the attacker, taking him down to the ground.

Relief spread over Jace, until he spied emerald-green eyes staring at him….

When Tala had scrambled around the corner and seen Jace on the ground and his attacker ready to deliver the lethal blow, she thought she'd died. Nothing could've prepared her for the pain, the horror—the rage. Instinct kicked in and she rushed the guy to stop him from killing Jace…her mate.

In that instant, she knew she loved him and she would fight the grim reaper himself for Jace's life.

As she tumbled on the ground with the misshapen attacker, Tala thought maybe that's who she was tangling with. For if he wasn't death, he was a darn close second with his dark, scaly skin, strange glowing eyes and sulfurous breath.

He tried to get a hold on her, but she was too swift, too agile. She squirmed and wriggled from his grip. He roared in frustration and made another lunge toward her. When he reared up on his hind legs, Tala moved in for the kill.

She leaped, staying low to the ground. Talons out, she swiped at his belly then twisted out of the way, rolling across the cement.

Sirens blared in the background as Tala leaped to her feet and waited for another attack. But it didn't come.

The attacker was gone. Vanished. Leaving only a blood trail that led, remarkably, up the side of the brick wall of the neighboring building.

Turning, Tala rushed to Jace's side. He had shifted back to human form and was lying in a pool of blood, his face slack and his eyes closed.

She nudged him with her nose, but he didn't stir. She had been too late.

Crouching onto her stomach beside Jace's body, Tala forced the change. Pain ripped and tore through her, but she didn't falter. She had to hurry. She had to save him at any cost.

Once transformed, she gathered him in her arms and pressed her lips to his forehead. Tears dripped from her eyes and splattered on his bloodied face. "No, God, no. Please, Jace, stay with me. Please." She rocked him back and forth, unsure of what to do.

Pressing her fingers to his neck, she found his pulse. It was slow but there. She didn't want to look at his injuries, knowing that they were savage and brutal, but she had to if she had any chance of helping him.

She surveyed his naked form. He was a bloody mess, but she could see where he had been ripped open. Along his ribs, there were several deep holes and tears. Blood continued to flow.

"Don't die on me, Jace," she murmured. "Not when I've just found you."

Tala looked around the alley, searching for anything she could use to staunch the flow of blood. But there was nothing but garbage and rustling papers. She was without clothing, having left that back at the apartment where she had shifted, so there was nothing on her she could use.

She only had herself, her hands.

Closing her eyes, she had a flash of the time when she was trying to shift and couldn't. Jace had laid his hands on her to help her through it. She had felt the warmth and power through his palms. Did she have that power? Could she heal Jace?

After cradling his head to the ground, Tala knelt along his side. She rubbed her hands together. Did she feel a spark of something?

Taking a deep breath, she laid them on Jace's body, over the two wounds high along his ribs. She squeezed her eyes shut and concentrated. And prayed.

Nothing happened.

Panic thrummed through her. She could barely breathe from the pressure in her chest. Opening her eyes, she glanced at his face. It was still slack and unresponsive. She checked his pulse again. It was there but fading.

Laying her hands on him again, she clamped her eyes shut and whispered, "I love you, Jace Jericho. Please, come back to me."

Slowly, warmth spread across her palms. She opened her eyes and watched in awe as her hands started to glow with a pale yellow light. Heat flared over her skin. It burned like dipping them into boiling water, but she didn't move, she didn't flinch. Tala kept her hands pressed firmly down on Jace's flesh.

She would heal him even if it killed her.

Opening her eyes, she watched, transfixed, as the oozing blood from his wounds stopped. She could almost see the flesh knitting back together. When he groaned, Tala lifted her hands from his body and set them on his face.

His eyelids fluttered open and the corners of his beautiful mouth lifted.

With tears streaming down her cheeks, she pressed her lips to his. "I thought I lost you."

"Never happen, babe," he croaked as he raised his hand and touched her cheek. "You saved me." He coughed.

"Don't talk. Help is coming." She smoothed her hand over his forehead and over his hair.

"Is he still here?"

She shook her head. "He's gone, but I hurt him."

"I knew you had it in you, babe. You're a lycan."

Somewhere inside Tala, a dam burst. Cradling his

head and shoulders in her lap, she hugged him close and sobbed. Emotions she didn't even know she harbored poured out of her in a rushing, soul-ripping stream.

She stayed like that, frozen in her pain, feeling the steady rhythm of his heart next to hers until hands lifted Jace from her lap and set him on a stretcher.

Chapter 31

The incessant beeping of the machines hooked up to his arm and chest was driving Jace mad. As were images of the previous night's violence.

He couldn't get his attacker's voice out of his head. On some level it rang eerily familiar to him, but it eluded him like a grain of salt on a beach.

All he wanted to do was rip the cords off, run out of the hospital and find Tala.

He hadn't heard from her since he'd been rushed to South Shadowwood in Necropolis. He'd been there under the doctor's all-seeing eye for the past twenty-four hours. That was long enough to be confined to a bed. Especially when there were other more interesting activities planned.

The curtain around his bed rustled. A plush wolf's head poked through the separated fabric.

"Hello, Jace, how are you today?" A muffled female voice sounded from behind the curtain.

His heart rate jumped and his stomach flipped over. Was Tala finally here to see him? To rescue him from this medical prison?

The curtain parted and Lyra stepped through, carrying the gray stuffed animal. "I brought you a friend to play with." She tossed him the toy.

He caught it and set it down along his side. "Thanks."

"How are you feeling?"

"I'm fine. I don't need to be here anymore." He rubbed his side where the holes in his flesh were already healed. They were still sore and achy, but definitely not life-threatening.

"Tell that to the doctor," she said.

"I have. Several times. But he's not listening."

Lyra sat on the edge of his bed and fiddled with the controls. The bed slowly rose higher, then lower. "The rest of the crew is coming. Caine just wanted to stop and talk to your doctor first."

"Everyone?" Jace asked, wincing at the eagerness in his voice.

Lyra glanced at him and gave him a small smile. She didn't need to say a word. It was written all over her face.

"I'm sorry, Jace."

He shook his head. "Doesn't matter."

"Maybe she's scared—"

"I said it doesn't matter."

Although it *did* matter, more than he was willing to admit. The pain of her abandonment ripped through his heart and tore up his soul. Rubbing a hand over his chest, he could still feel the bond. It thumped and pulsed like a living, breathing entity. He knew it would never vanish but hoped that in time it would fade into the background.

He heard a few people enter his room. It afforded him enough time to hide his feelings. He was acting like a sissy. He'd be damned if he'd let anyone else see it.

He raised his chin before the curtain was dragged open to reveal Caine, Eve and, surprisingly, Hector smiling at him.

"There he is," Caine said. "Our two-hundred-pound bundle of joy."

"Get me the hell out of here, Chief," Jace growled.

"The doc says you can leave in a few hours. He's just going over the last of your tests. Everything appears normal and you're healing fine."

"I could've told him that."

Everyone laughed.

Eve stepped up to his bed, leaned over and planted a kiss to his forehead. "I'm happy to see you grumbling again." She quickly moved back and wrapped her arm around Caine. He pressed his lips to the top of her head, as he always did.

The kiss and sentiment surprised Jace. Eve and he had never been too friendly. But maybe things were starting to change. There'd been a lot of that happening lately. To the team, to him.

Glancing at Hector, seeing his smiling face in an Otherworld hospital, proved that fact even more. He wondered how the human even got permission to enter the city, let alone come and see him.

"I wanted to thank you for all the work you did on this case. We couldn't have done it without you and your gifts."

Jace nodded. Words seemed to be having difficulty forming in his throat. Emotion clamped around him again. Damn it! He was becoming an overly sensitive nitwit.

"We got Darryl with enough evidence to try him for all three murders," Hector continued.

"That's good to hear."

"We found the rope, and hook he used to cut the first victim's throat." Hector went on. "His boot tread also matched the print you found at the house."

Jace nodded. "What about the second victim?"

"We located a rusty razor blade in the trunk of his car. It had the victim's blood on it."

"Did he say what he used the blood for?"

Hector shook his head. "That, we don't know. But at least the families can have their justice."

Justice. That was something Jace definitely wanted. Memories of the beast he'd fought in the alley came flooding back to him. "Any word on what exactly I came up against? It seemed like it was part vamp, part lycan, part something else entirely." He took in a ragged breath. "I can still smell the sulfur."

"Gwen's working overtime to analyze the blood and the skin scrapings we collected from your fight," Caine said. "We'll find the answer."

"Rick's been helping her," Hector added. "He says it's his new mission in life."

Jace smiled, remembering the spunky young human technician.

Caine squeezed Jace's leg through the blanket. Jace knew it was his friend's way of offering comfort. Words would never pass between the two. That was not how their dynamic worked.

After patting Jace once more, Caine put his arm around Eve and smiled. "Okay, my friend. We'll leave so you can get some rest before the doc springs you. I'll call you later. Take a few days off at least."

"Do I get paid?"

Caine chuckled. "I'll take it under consideration." With a final tip of his head, Caine and Eve turned to exit the room.

Lyra grabbed Jace's hand, squeezed it, then let go and followed the others out the door.

Hector came around the side of the bed. He slid an envelope out of his jacket pocket and handed it to Jace. "She wanted me to give this to you."

Jace took the manila envelope and stared at Tala's handwriting. *Jace* it read simply. Turning it in his fingers, he could feel his chest tightening.

"I wanted you to know that I'll keep her secret. It's up to her what she plans on doing with it."

Jace met the man's gaze and nodded. "You're a good man, Hector. I'd work with you anytime."

"You, as well."

They shook hands, then Hector left him with his letter from Tala.

His hands shook when he opened it, unfolded the light blue paper and saw her elegant handwriting. He held it to his nose and breathed in her spicy scent. His body twitched in response. For as long as he lived, he'd never forget her smell.

Dear Jace,

I have a lot of things I want to say to you, but not the right words to say them. You deserve so much more than this letter.

So much more than me.

You nearly died because of my inability to accept my true self. I'll never forgive myself for that.

Please don't contact me. Move on with your life, Jace. Find your one true mate and be happy.
Always,
Tala

He read her words twice before folding the paper and sliding it back into the envelope.

Jace wanted to yell, he wanted to rant and rage. And he wanted to shake Tala and tell her that there was no one else for him. That she, despite everything she felt about herself, was the only woman for him. Forever.

Ripping the monitors off his chest and yanking the IV from his hand, Jace swung his legs off the bed and stood. Enough lying around. Enough feeling sorry for himself. If he wanted something, damn it, he'd go out and get it.

Jace stomped out of his room and into the sterile white hallway. As he stalked toward the nurses' station, he had a passing thought that his bare butt was most likely peeking out between the barely tied parts of his blue hospital gown. He didn't care. If people wanted to look, they could have a nice long gaze for all that mattered to him.

He just wanted a damn phone.

That luxury had been conveniently left out of his room. It didn't really surprise him, as his usual hospital stays had been less than twenty-four hours due to extraordinary healing powers.

When he approached the triage desk, the two nurses on duty regarded him with a mixture of caution and curiosity. The cautious one was a vampire and the other a lycan like himself. He could smell her growing attraction as he drew near.

"I need a phone."

Arching a brow, the vampire lifted her finely boned hand to point down the hall. "There's a pay phone down there."

He growled. "Does it look like I'm carrying any change?"

The lycan nurse chuckled and pushed the phone on the counter toward him "Knock yourself out, Mr. Jericho."

Snatching up the receiver, Jace punched in Tala's home phone number. Fear of losing her and anger from her rejection warred in his mind as the phone rang. After three rings the answering machine picked up. With Tala's melodic voice announcing her failure to be available singing in his ears, he lost all his ability to talk. What the hell was he going to say?

The beep sounded and his tongue went numb, sticking to the roof of his mouth. It didn't help that the nurses and other patients passing the triage desk were staring at him.

Turning from their gazes, he cupped his hand around the receiver. "Tala, its Jace. Hector gave me your letter. I, ah, just wanted to say that you are so much more than you think. And I'd be dead if you hadn't showed up." He shook his head and swore under his breath. This is not what he wanted to say. His emotions were brimming at the surface, ready to spill over.

"Damn it, woman. Listen to me. I'd be dead without you." Not sure what else he could say, Jace placed the receiver back into the cradle and slowly walked back to his room. His chest ached and he knew it had nothing to do with his physical wounds.

Chapter 32

Tala stared at her answering machine with tears brimming in her eyes as she listened to Jace's message. She could hear the anguish and anger in his voice and she desperately wanted to reach through the lines and touch him. If only one last time.

She hadn't been expecting it. She hadn't thought he'd call her after reading her note. That he would slice at her heart and soul. A razor blade carving into her pain.

When the message ended, she stared at the phone, willing it to ring again. Maybe if Jace called again, she'd change her mind. Maybe hearing his deep, sexy voice warming her ear would alter her plans. Maybe it would give her a reason to follow her heart instead of her head.

She nearly jumped out of her skin when the phone trilled. She reached for it, then hesitated like a coward, letting the machine pick up.

"I delivered the note."

Hector's voice rumbled through the speaker. She snatched up the receiver and put it to her ear. "I'm here."

"I gave Jace the letter."

"I know." Tala squeezed the phone tight as she stared out her bedroom window and traced the outline of the moon with her finger on the glass. "Thank you, Hector, for giving it to him." She paused, then continued, "How is he?"

"He's healed and already fighting to get out of bed."

She smiled. "That's good."

"Are you sure you're making the right decision, Tala? Leaving the force and moving away just doesn't make sense. You have other choices."

"Thanks again, Hector. For that and for keeping my secret. I appreciate it. I'll call you when I relocate."

"He loves you, you know."

Sighing, she rubbed a hand over the throb in her chest. "I know. I'll talk to you soon." Hanging up, she set the phone on her dresser.

The moon winked at Tala as she stared out into the night. She'd been silver-free for going on three days now, and the moon called to her like a siren's sweet song.

She wanted to run.

Even after having more silver nitrate made, she had

yet to use any. Something stayed her hand. The thing that sparked and flared under her breastbone. The bond between her and Jace. She wondered how far she'd have to travel before it would finally break.

Pulling herself away from the window, Tala moved to her closet and took down the boxes and other miscellaneous items sitting on the top shelf.

It had been more than five years since she'd gone through this stuff. Some of it might have even been her mother's. Tala had stored some of Claudia's things when she had moved from her house to her new apartment.

After taping together some new boxes, Tala busied herself with tossing shoes, jackets and other clothing into them. Anything to keep her mind off Jace.

She wondered what he was doing. Had he been released from the hospital yet? Was he running through his favorite park, soaking up the glorious rays of moonlight? Did he think of her?

Those were the exact thoughts she was trying to avoid, but they were solidly lodged in her head. That and the image of a bloodied and bruised Jace lying in her arms.

She didn't think that image would ever go away. It would haunt her for the rest of her life no matter how far she ran to try to erase it.

Shaking her head to dislodge the thought, Tala taped up one box, then sat down on the rug and went about going through the tedious task of sorting through the various junk boxes. She opened one and started to take out the stuff inside —her mother's things.

She ran her hand over a wooden music jewelry box. She remembered all the times she'd played dress up with her mother's necklaces and rings while the pretty music played in the background. Smiling, Tala continued to poke through the contents of the box and picked up a stack of what looked like letters bound together with a red ribbon.

Flipping through them, she saw that they were all from the same person. Maybe her mother had a secret love.

Curious, Tala slipped one letter out at random, opened it and began to read.

My Dearest Claudia,
It was with a sad heart that I received your letter.
Love always,
J.D.

After Tala read the letter, she scrambled for another. Opening it, she read it over quickly, every word making her ill. She felt as if she were in quicksand, being sucked into oblivion.

Tossing the second letter aside, she opened another, then another. The words and their meaning swirled around in her head, making her dizzy. She gasped for breath....

I'll always love you...my condition...a child...don't leave me... Forever...

J.D....

Her mother had lied to her. Lies so treacherous she thought she was going to get sick.

Unable to move even when she heard her front door

open and close, Tala sat on the rug, her knees up to her chest, and held the last letter in her hand.

A letter from her father.

"There you are, dear," Claudia said as she walked into Tala's bedroom. "I phoned earlier, but you didn't—"

Tala raised her head and glared at her mother. "Why?"

Claudia's face paled as she saw what Tala was reading. Walking to the bed, she sat on the edge but said nothing.

"You lied to me, Mother."

"I did what was best for you, Tala. You have to understand that."

Crumpling the letter in her fist, Tala jumped to her feet. "I *don't* understand. How could you make me believe that my father was a rapist? How is that better for me?"

"I didn't want you to grow up in that environment, Tala. For you to have to deal with the prejudice and hatred of being one of them."

Tala swirled around and screamed, "I *am* one of them!"

Standing, Claudia reached out to Tala. But Tala shrugged from her touch. She couldn't stand to be touched by her, not after all the lies she had told over the years. All the guilt and shame she had heaped onto Tala rather than deal with who she was.

"I'm a lycan, whether you want me to be or not. Keeping me away from my father didn't change that."

"I didn't keep you from him," Claudia said as she wrapped her arms around herself. "He could've come to see you. He could've sent me money to help raise you."

Tala shook her head, anger swelling over her. "I read

the letters, Mother. You told him not to contact you, not to ever come near you. You even threatened him with exposure if he tried."

"I couldn't have you growing up like that, Tala. I just couldn't. It wouldn't have been fair."

"Fair to whom?" Tala bit out. "Fair to you? You didn't want the burden of raising a child that was different. You didn't want to face the stares and whispers from the other mothers on the playground, is that it? Well, I am different, Mother. And there is nothing you can do about it. Not then, not now."

Claudia turned and walked to the window. She leaned against the wall and stared outside. "He never told me what he was, Tala. Not the entire three months we dated. Not until I was pregnant."

Tala didn't want to feel any sympathy for her mother. She had lied to her. Lies that had caused Tala to hate herself, to hate what she genetically couldn't fight. But still a pang of sadness filled her heart with what her mother must have gone through.

"He was such a beautiful man," Claudia uttered. "I was so in love with him."

"Then why did you push him away?"

Claudia whirled around, and the look on her face told Tala everything she needed to know.

"Because he was a—an animal. How can you love a beast like that?" she sneered.

Angry tears rolled down Tala's cheeks. "Then how can you love me?"

"I tried my best with you. I really did."

"Well, your best isn't good enough. Not anymore. Not for me." Turning on her heel, Tala marched out of her bedroom.

Claudia followed her into the living room. "Where are you going?"

Tala grabbed her jacket and car keys. "To get what I deserve."

Without another word, she walked out the door. The moment she stepped outside, Tala felt a great weight lift from her shoulders. As if she had finally sloughed off the one thing that had been keeping her from true happiness.

Chapter 33

Sweat ran down his body as Jace stepped out of the trees near his house. He had gone for a long strenuous run hoping to mask the pain in his chest with another type of agony. It hadn't helped.

He had gone into the lab earlier to help wrap up the loose ends on the murders in San Antonio, but Caine had promptly told him to go home, as they had it all taken care of. The evidence on Darryl Rockland had stuck like glue and the prosecutors were satisfied with what they had to go to court. There'd been no more murders or sightings of any strange creatures running around town.

Everything had been taken care of. Everything except the pain in his heart.

Thoughts and images of Tala still raced through his mind.

As he crossed the street, he sensed he was being watched. Glancing both ways along the road, he couldn't see anyone. Many of his neighbors, lycans mostly, were out for their own runs. The few vampires that lived down the block worked nights, so they wouldn't likely be home, either.

He turned and stared into the trees. No glowing eyes shone back at him. There was nothing but the raccoons, rodents and other animals who lived in the surrounding park.

He scented the air, but no odd smell came to him, just the usual pleasant night odors. If he was being watched, whoever it was stood downwind from him.

He was still wary from his battle with whatever it was. The sensation of being watched wasn't necessarily menacing. If it was the creature from the alley, Jace would certainly feel it. A person didn't stare into those strange glowing eyes and not know the face of death. He'd know it if he was looking into it again.

Jace continued across the street, up his steps and through his front door. He never locked it. He didn't think there was anyone stupid enough to break into his house. He had nothing of value anyway. Once inside, he shut the door behind him and froze.

Tala's scent floated around him, instantly intoxicating him.

"Ah, I'm sorry. The door was unlocked." From her

stance at the window, she averted her gaze, but he saw her cheeks redden before she could fully turn away. Now he knew who'd been watching him in the street.

She was making a conscious effort not to look at his nakedness. His ego inflated when he spied her sneaking peeks at him as he walked across the room.

Snatching his sweatpants from the floor where he had tossed them earlier, Jace slid them on. "Do you always break into people's houses?"

"No, but technically, since your door was unlocked, I didn't break in." She moved to the sofa and sat.

"Okay, so you got me there." He wandered into the kitchen and opened his refrigerator door. Anything to occupy his hands and his brain. He was unprepared to see her, especially in his house.

Grabbing two bottles of beer, he popped their caps and carried them back into the living room. He handed her one, then sat on the chair opposite the sofa. Jace took a long pull, then looked at her.

She stared at the bottle in her hand. Sadness and regret wafted off her. It broke his heart all over again to feel those sensations from her.

"My father's name is J. D. Black." She tipped the beer to her mouth and took a long drink.

"What? I thought—"

"For my entire life, my mother has lied to me." Tala glanced up at him. He could see the hurt in her eyes. The betrayal.

Setting his beer down on the table, Jace moved over

to the sofa and sat beside her. Not so close as to invade her space, but close enough for her to know that she could reach out to him if she wished.

She shook her head. "She told me that he had raped her. That she never truly knew who he was. And the whole time she knew exactly who and what he was. She had even loved him once. Before she found out that he was a lycan, of course." She took another pull on the beer. "But then it was too late. She was already pregnant with his beastly child."

"How did you find out?"

"I found his letters to her. Letters full of love and anguish. He wanted me, Jace. He wanted to know me so much." Tears rolled down her cheeks.

He couldn't stand to see them on her beautiful face. Moving closer to her, he wiped her tears away with his thumb. "Of course he wanted you, darling. Look at you. You're a work of perfection."

The corners of her mouth lifted in a soft but sad smile. She turned to him and touched his hand on her face. "Will you…" She paused, her throat working overtime swallowing what he knew to be tears. "Will you help me find him?"

"Of course. Whatever you need. If he's around I'll find him."

"Thank you. You're a good friend." Her smile blossomed and he dropped his hand, now unsure what to do or what to say. He didn't want to be just a good friend. He wanted to be her one and only, her everything.

But how could he ask for that after what she'd just been through? It seemed so selfish. He had so many things he wanted to tell her, but he was afraid of scaring her. She was here in his home, asking for his help. Maybe it would be enough. Maybe he could live with just that.

Wiping away the last of her tears, she said, "I quit my job."

"You did?"

"Yes, and I plan on moving."

He sat back on the sofa. His heart was racing. He didn't want her to move away. She had already been too far from him living in San Antonio. What if she moved to another state?

"You're leaving San Antonio?"

She nodded. "I can't stay there anymore. It's too difficult with all that's happened. I need to get away. To think. To heal."

He couldn't do it. There was no way he could let her go. Not now. He'd wither away into ash if he had to watch her walk away.

"Move here, to Necropolis," he blurted out. Leaning forward, he grabbed her hands in his. "I have enough room for the two of us. It's close to a beautiful park. I can teach you about using and controlling your gift. And the pack will love you. I promise you'd never feel out of place again."

"I don't know, Jace. We hardly know each other."

He could feel her pulling away. Panic gripped him tightly. He couldn't lose her. Not again.

Lifting her hand, he pressed it to his chest. "I know everything I need to know about you in here, Tala. You are special to me. More important than any woman has been."

"You're special to me, too, Jace, but can that be enough?"

"I've been restless all my life. Searching for the one person to complete my soul. I found that someone. You."

She shook her head and chewed on her bottom lip. He had to make her understand how he felt.

"Damn it, woman, are you not listening to me? I love you and I won't let you go. What do you think about that?"

Tala smiled. "Promise?"

His eyes bugged out. "What?"

She laid a hand on his cheek. "The entire time I was arguing with my mother, all I could think about was seeing you. How I knew you would make the pain go away as if it had never existed. You've healed me from the inside out."

Tala pressed her lips to his in a slow, wet passionate kiss that he wanted to drown himself in.

"I promise. No matter how much you squirm, you're not getting away from me. Ever."

"I love you, Jace. You're the only one for me."

He pulled her to him and covered her mouth with his again. The kiss was everything he felt about her. Hot, fiery and forever.

Jace jumped to his feet and pulled her up. Bending, he grabbed her by the legs and tossed her over his shoulder.

"What are you doing?"

"Sealing the deal." He carried her across the living room and into his bedroom. He tossed her onto his bed.

"Sealing the deal?"

He grabbed one of her legs and peeled off her shoe and sock. "Yes, this is how lycans negotiate and confirm the end of a deal."

"Is that right?"

"Oh, yeah." He lifted her T-shirt over her head and tossed it across the room. "You have a lot to learn about lycan behavior."

"Yes, I'm beginning to believe that." She laughed when he gripped her pants and tore them down her legs. "So, you're going to teach me?"

Nodding, Jace slid his thumbs into his sweatpants and pulled them down his legs. He stepped out of them and kicked the pants into a corner.

"Lesson number one." Growling, he leaned over her and pushed her back onto the mattress. "How to please your mate. For the rest of her life."

"Sounds promising. Can't wait to hear about lesson two." Wrapping her arms around him, she pulled Jace down to her body. "I think I'm ready to get started."

Instantly warmth spread over him. A pleasing, perfect heat that radiated from the top of his head to the tips of his toes. He had never felt more at home in his life. He had found his one true mate.

* * * * *

*Mills & Boon® Intrigue brings you
a sneak preview of...*

Linda Conrad's The Sheriff's Amnesiac Bride

*When a woman on the run shows up in his life, Sheriff
Jericho Yates takes her in. The trouble is, she can't
remember who she is or why someone was shooting
at her! As "Rosie" and Jericho uncover bits about her
past, they must dodge the goons who are after her, all
while trying to ignore their undeniable attraction...*

*Don't miss this thrilling new story available next
month from Mills & Boon® Intrigue.*

The Sheriff's Amnesiac Bride
by
Linda Conrad

Still twisting her hands in the backseat and waiting for a good opportunity, the woman with no past and a questionable future bit her lip and stared out the car's window. There was so much traffic here. Surely one of the people in these other cars would see her predicament and come to her aid.

"Son of a bitch, the traffic's even worse now." The car wound down to a crawl as the driver turned around again to speak to her. "Don't get smart, lady. You call out or make any noises like you need help and we'll shoot you. I don't give a rat's damn if that special item the boss wants is ever found or not. The choice between you giving us the answer and you never being able to answer again ain't nothing to me.

"You got that?"

She nodded, but the movement seared a line of fiery pain down her temple. Another couple of pains like that and she might rather be dead anyway.

"Terrific," the goon sitting shotgun said. "Just look at that, will ya? A local smoky. Out in the middle of the highway, directing traffic. Crap.

"What's going to happen, Arnie?" The man in the passenger seat was beginning to sweat.

"We're not doing anything wrong," Arnie answered with a growl. "We're regular citizens just driving down the road. Nothing to worry about. Stash your gun under the seat until we pass him by."

The driver bent and buried his own gun, then twisted back to her. "Remember, sis. No funny stuff. I swear, if you call out, you're dead."

Shaking badly, she wondered if her voice would work anyway. But right then, the miracle she'd prayed for happened. Their car came to a complete stop, almost directly in front of the church.

She bit her lip and tried to guess whether it would be closer for her to head for the sanctuary of the church or to run for the policeman in the street ten car-lengths away. The truck in front of them inched ahead and she decided to break for the church—it was her only real choice.

For a split second she stopped to wonder if she might be the kind of person who made rash decisions and who would rather fight back than die with a whimper. But then, whether out of fear or out of instinct, she knew it didn't matter.

If she were ever going to find out what had happened to her in the first place, she would have to go. Now.

* * *

Jericho heard a popping sound behind his back. Spinning around, he scanned the area trying to make out where the noise had originated.

"Was that a gunshot?" Fisher asked, as he too checked out the scene in front of the church.

In his peripheral vision, Jericho spotted a woman he'd never seen before. A woman seemingly out of place for a wedding, dressed in fancy jeans and red halter top. And she was racing at top speed across the grass straight in his direction. What the hell?

Another pop and the woman fell on the concrete walkway. From off to his left, someone screamed. Then tires squealed from somwhere down the long line of cars. When he glanced toward the sound, he saw a sedan with two men sitting in front as they roared out of the line and headed down the narrow shoulder of the highway.

Chaos reigned. Car horns honked. People shouted. And the sedan spewed out a huge dust plume as it bumped down the embankment.

Jericho took off at a run. He dropped to one knee beside the woman, checked her pulse and discovered she was breathing but unconscious and bleeding.

"Is she alive?" Deputy Rawlins asked, almost out of breath as he came running up. "I got their plates, Sheriff. But I didn't dare get off a shot with all the civilians in the way. You want me to pursue?"

Son of a gun. It would figure that he didn't have his weapon just when an emergency arose.

"Stay with the woman," Jericho ordered. "You and

Fisher get her to Doc O'Neal's as fast as you can. My rifle's in the truck, and…" He looked over his shoulder toward the church door. "Tell Macy…"

Right then Macy appeared at the top of the church steps and peered down at him. He was about to yell for her to get back out of the line of fire. But within a second, he could see her quickly taking in the whole situation.

"You go do what you need to, Jericho," she called out to him. "Don't worry about us. Just take care of yourself. The wedding's off for today."

INTRIGUE

Coming next month

2-IN-1 ANTHOLOGY

THE SHERIFF'S AMNESIAC BRIDE by Linda Conrad

When a woman on the run shows up in his life, Sheriff Jericho Yates takes her in. Even if she can't remember who she is or why she is a hitman's target…

SOLDIER'S SECRET CHILD by Caridad Piñeiro

They'd shared one night of passion eighteen years ago, but Macy Ward had never told sexy military man Fisher about the consequences!

2-IN-1 ANTHOLOGY

QUESTIONING THE HEIRESS by Delores Fossen

Texas Ranger Egan is the one man socialite Caroline can turn to, yet now he's spearheading an investigation that may uncover the dark past they share…

DAREDEVIL'S RUN by Kathleen Creighton

After a tragic accident rugged Matt shunned his fiancée and business partner, Alex. But can he find a way to let her back into his heart?

SINGLE TITLE

UNBOUND by Lori Devoti
Nocturne

Risk is a hell-hound, doomed to shapeshift between human and canine form, until he meets witch Kara, the one woman who can break his curse.

On sale 21st August 2009

Available at WHSmith, Tesco, ASDA, Eason and all good bookshops.
For full Mills & Boon range including eBooks visit
www.millsandboon.co.uk

INTRIGUE

Coming next month

2-IN-1 ANTHOLOGY

HER BEST FRIEND'S HUSBAND by Justine Davis

Gabriel's wife disappeared eight years ago. Now he's falling for her best friend – yet could his newfound feelings for Cara help him uncover a dark, dramatic truth?

THE BEAST WITHIN by Lisa Renee Jones

Jag was torn from his wife, Caren – and the mortal realm – by the soulless Darkland Beasts. Resurrected, he will stop at nothing to recover the love he lost!

SINGLE TITLE

THE MYSTERY MAN OF WHITEHORSE by BJ Daniels

Laci can't keep her eyes off her new boss, mysterious and brooding Bridger. Yet his timely arrival also provides a clue in the murders that haunt the town of Whitehorse.

SINGLE TITLE

PRIVATE S.W.A.T TAKEOVER by Julie Miller

When Liza witnessed the murder of KCPD's deputy commissioner, top cop Holden was appointed her official protector – but falling for her wasn't part of the bargain!

On sale 4th September 2009

Available at WHSmith, Tesco, ASDA, Eason and all good bookshops.
For full Mills & Boon range including eBooks visit
www.millsandboon.co.uk

From No. 1 *New York Times* bestselling author Nora Roberts

Night Shift available 7th August 2009

When her stalker's threats start to escalate, late-night DJ Cilla O'Roarke and Detective Boyd Fletcher are led into a terrifying situation that they might not both walk away from…

Night Shadow available 4th September 2009

Faced with a choice between her own life and the law, can prosecutor Deborah O'Roarke make the right decision – before someone else dies?

**Passion. Power. Suspense.
It's time to fall under the spell
of Nora Roberts.**

Rich, successful and gorgeous...

These Australian men clearly need wives!

Featuring:

THE WEALTHY AUSTRALIAN'S PROPOSAL
by Margaret Way

THE BILLIONAIRE CLAIMS HIS WIFE
by Amy Andrews

INHERITED BY THE BILLIONAIRE
by Jennie Adams

Available 21st August 2009

www.millsandboon.co.uk

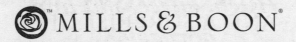

2 FREE BOOKS
AND A SURPRISE GIFT

We would like to take this opportunity to thank you for reading this Mills & Boon® book by offering you the chance to take TWO more specially selected titles from the Intrigue series absolutely FREE! We're also making this offer to introduce you to the benefits of the Mills & Boon® Book Club™—

- **FREE home delivery**
- **FREE gifts and competitions**
- **FREE monthly Newsletter**
- **Exclusive Mills & Boon Book Club offers**
- **Books available before they're in the shops**

Accepting these FREE books and gift places you under no obligation to buy, you may cancel at any time, even after receiving your free books. Simply complete your details below and return the entire page to the address below. You don't even need a stamp!

YES Please send me 2 free Intrigue books and a surprise gift. I understand that unless you hear from me, I will receive 5 superb new titles every month, including two 2-in-1 titles priced at £4.99 each and a single title priced at £3.19, postage and packing free. I am under no obligation to purchase any books and may cancel my subscription at any time. The free books and gift will be mine to keep in any case.

Ms/Mrs/Miss/Mr _____ initials _____

Surname _____
address _____

_____

_____ postcode _____

Send this whole page to: Mills & Boon Book Club, Free Book Offer, FREEPOST NAT 10298, Richmond, TW9 1BR